THE LYNCHERS

THE LYNCHERS

Steven C. Lawrence

GUNSMOKE

First published in the UK by Ace Books

This hardback edition 2011
by AudioGO Ltd
by arrangement with
Golden West Literary Agency

ISBN 978 1 445 85651 3

British Library Cataloguing in Publication Data available.

Printed and bound in Great Britain by
MPG Books Group Limited

Chapter One

That Thursday evening in July, the town of Gunnison should have been dozing in dusty silence. It was after six-thirty and the business day was through. The sun's heat was abating, and the wide shadows of the west side false fronts made their slow, steady crawl toward the opposite boardwalks.

But the people weren't at their supper tables as usual. Home from work, the town men, the merchants who owned the stores, the railroaders from the depot and the roundhouse, and the laborers of the section all had herded their families into their houses after the young Jensen kid had ridden in pushing his horse at a dead run. Even the cowhands who lived in town but hired out to MacCandles had been let off early once the word had been spread that Slattery was coming back. At a time like this, when no one knew exactly what might happen, MacCandles had made it plain he believed a man was needed by and belonged with his family.

Byron Foye, whose blacksmith shop sat on the eastern edge of the broad Nebraska flat, was the first one to see him. Foye was a huge whiskered man with tremendous arms and shoulders. Though he'd made Grace and the two girls go into the back room of their house and stay there, Foye had kept up his work on the twisted wagon iron he was pounding into shape.

He'd given the red-hot iron its final blows when he glanced up from the anvil. Beyond the shed the hazy dusk seemed to come from the Platte as sunset faded, leaving a soft, blue darkness over the river. Foye lifted one hairy arm to wipe the sweat from his forehead, and he saw the horse and rider break from the willow thicket onto the high sandy left bank.

Foye set down the tongs and hammer, stepped quickly through the back of the shed to the house. "Grace," he called. "Grace."

"Yes." The word was muffled behind the thick wood, yet he could tell she was still nerved up.

"He's comin' now," Foye told her calmly. "Call over to Tupper's and have them pass the word to the Bromleys."

He didn't wait for an answer, just moved back into the shed. His old Spencer rifle was in the rear of the front stall, leaned against the corner. Foye picked up the weapon, checked its load. He had nothing personal against Slattery, and like many of the people here, he'd felt there had been something wrong at the trial. But for the past five years Foye had had things better than he'd ever known them in his life. Jim MacCandles had made that for him. He'd made it for the town. There was only one place Foye could stand if shooting started, and that was with MacCandles.

Tom Slattery swung his black gelding wide to

the right, away from the willows and cottonwoods and onto the newly built dirt road, parallel to the railroad. He'd stayed close to the river for the last ten miles. He'd accepted the great cloud of mosquitoes which hummed along the greyish-white sandbars that thrust out into the sluggish, gurgling current as part of the price of riding in without being seen. Now, his eyes on the empty walks and porches ahead, and the closed windows and doors, usually kept open to catch the coolness of the night breeze, he knew he had no advantage after all.

Light pressure from Slattery's knees made the gelding slow its walk even more. His hard eyes were cautious and his big body remained slightly hunched as his right hand dropped and patted the horse's neck. "Easy now, boy," he said. "You'll be in your own stall tonight." The hand raised again. The fingers touched the front button of his black coat, flicking it open to expose the bone handle of the Navy Colt that jutted out above the waistband of his trousers.

Slattery was large and deep-chested, in his middle thirties. The look of a tough and capable man rode on his weather-burned, stubbled face. His coat and denim trousers, held into tight cylindrical shapes where they were drawn over high-heeled boots, had a newness to them; still they showed he'd been riding a good long distance. The hand which had unbuttoned the coat didn't move with the motion of the horse, but stayed calm and poised, an equal distance between the Colt's butt and the stock of a Winchester rifle booted in the

7

long shiny leather beneath his right knee.

Once past the ramshackle blacksmith's shed he could see fully how Gunnison had grown the last five years. New two-story buildings had replaced the storage sheds between the business district and the residential section of the upper town. A block beyond the sheriff's office, there was a bank now, made of red bricks which must have been freighted in. More homes had been built too—substantial white painted houses with big half-glass doors that glared fiery reddish-orange in the last traces of the sunlight.

It was a far cry from the straggling line of flimsy wooden buildings he and his brother and father had found in seventy-one when they'd staked out their land, nothing more than shacks thrown up by the saloon keepers, gamblers and storekeepers to get the trade of the men who were trying to build their ranches here. And it was a far cry from the small town where his father and brother had been killed and he'd been beaten senseless by a wild mob and then tried and sentenced for five to ten years in the Federal prison at Omaha.

Thinking of that he could feel his tenseness coming back. He flexed his fingers, letting them rest against the saddle horn. Then, when he saw the screen door of Bromley's Hotel swing out, his hand relaxed.

The man in the lead he knew, but Slattery didn't tie Horse Owens in with MacCandles. He was a huge, deceptively fat man whose round childish face masked a bullyish arrogance. The one behind him was younger than Horse, lean and muscular, with a tight mouth and blank, cunning eyes. They were not eyes that went with the cowhand's clothing he wore. His gun was thonged low and tight to his right thigh so even moving slowly the tips of his fingers brushed its black handle.

Both halted at the center of the porch steps. They blocked the doorway, openly hostile while they watched Slattery dismount at the hotel hitchrail and tie a halter knot around the worn wood.

Slattery took his time unloading his blanket roll, glanced back along Center Street, catching the shadows that moved behind curtained windows and in the cover of the doorways. He hefted the roll onto his left shoulder and started up the hotel steps.

Owens puffed out his chest. Both large hands were doubled into fists. He coughed, rubbed his jaw with his right knuckles.

"Where you figure you're goin', Slattery?" he questioned.

"You own the hotel now?"

"No."

"Then I haven't any business with you."

The giant sniffed, shifted his weight. He stared down his wide nose at Slattery. "You're goin' after young Bromley for testifyin' against you. Well, you're goin' no farther." He shifted his hobnailed boots again, ready to charge down the stairs. His companion edged to the side, watching patiently.

"I'm not after anyone. Not here," Slattery said. He balanced the roll, his grip loosening. From the corner of his eye he saw a shadow appear in the dust on the right, then lengthen into the form of a man. He swung calmly around, let his fingers flip open his coat.

"Hold it, Tom."

Slattery's hand paused at the sound of Sheriff Gus Loheed's voice. The lawman walked past him and up onto the second step, putting himself between Slattery and Owens. He was still tall and straight, with a mustache, fiftyish; but he was a changed person from the man Slattery remembered. His once solid build was covered by a flabbiness, and his clothes fit awkwardly, too small in the shoulders and arms, as if cut for another man.

"You come here for trouble, Tom?"

"No trouble. Not now. I just want to hire a room and leave my things. And to talk to some people."

"Freddy Bromley?"

Slattery nodded calmly. "The boy's older now, Gus. But that's all I want to do. Talk to him."

Owens' boots creaked and Loheed glanced up at him. "I'll handle this, Horse."

"We ain't goin' to let him touch Freddy, Sheriff."

"I'll handle it," Loheed repeated. He spat a mouthful of tobacco juice as his eyes flicked up and down the street. Doors had opened and men had appeared. A few had already come onto the walks, slowly, uncertainly. Loheed motioned to Slattery.

"I'll take your gun," he ordered. "There's a

no-gun law here now." He held out his right hand, reached up with the left and drew the Winchester from its boot. "Hand it over."

Slattery's face showed nothing. His eyes roamed beyond the lawman to the approaching men. Across on the porch of the general store a woman had come outside with her husband. He was trying to leave her and join the spectators, but she pulled at his shirt sleeve with her hand and pleaded fearfully with him. Slattery's gaze went to the weapons Owens and his companion wore.

"What is it?" he asked. "A special law."

"Horse and Gillman have permits. They don't have to answer to you. I'll take that gun. Right now, Tom."

The men were closer; many gathered together into small groups while they crowded in to hear. Most of the faces were familiar, especially the older ones who'd come out of the houses, but neither MacCandles nor any of his riders were present. Slattery heard someone snap an obscene curse. He gave it no notice. He drew the Colt from his waistband and handed it to Loheed.

"That all, Gus?"

"Just as long as you don't push trouble. No trouble at all."

Slattery gazed around at the circle of watching faces, all looking quiet and angry, hearing the small mutter that ran through the rear of the crowd. He nodded to Loheed slowly. Then, taking a firm grip on the blanket roll he went up the stairs, past Owens, and pulled open the screen door.

The hotel lobby was wide and high-ceilinged. The warm, good smell of fried steak and potatoes lingered in the comparatively cool air of the room. Martin Bromley waited behind the registration desk. He was a gray-haired man of about sixty, coatless, the sleeves of his white shirt tucked under black garters. He didn't move his eyes from Slattery's face while Slattery walked past the leather divan and chairs spotted neatly about the carpetless hardwood floor. The large coal-oil lamp over the key rack threw flickering shadows across the desk and the ancient lithographs on the walls gave a worried, sunken expression to his wrinkled features. He spoke out before Slattery reached the counter.

"There's no room for you in here. You turn around and find someplace else."

Slattery stopped at the desk and leaned the roll against the wall. He took off his flat-crowned hat, wiped his forehead with the side of his sleeve. "I didn't come back to make trouble for you, Mr. Bromley."

"You want to make trouble for my son. I don't want you in my hotel." At the sound of a door opening somewhere along the hall to the left, he placed both hands palm down on the counter, as though he was bracing himself. "You don't get out, I'll call for Loheed."

Slattery felt a sudden surge of anger grip him, at the sheriff's disarming him and at Bromley's unwillingness to even listen. The rustle of a dress came from the hallway, and Bromley's wife appeared. She was a thin, sharp-nosed woman who carried her head high.

"Don't waste time, Martin," she said. "You've told him you don't want him here. Get the sheriff."

Slattery offered quietly, "Mrs. Bromley. I didn't come back to harm Freddy."

"You did. You said you'd get the men who put you behind bars. My son was the principal witness against you and you're after him."

"No, Mrs. Bromley. I received a letter from Freddy last month. I just want to talk to him." He began to reach into his inner coat pocket.

The woman threw her hands up to her face and gasped. "He's got a gun, Martin." Her voice raised. "Sheriff. Sheriff!"

Stunned, Slattery dropped his hand, said fast, "The sheriff's got my gun. I want to show . . ."

"You won't show me anything. My son never wrote you a letter. He told the truth in court." Her stare flashed to the screen door as it swung inward and banged against the wall. Loheed ran in, holding Slattery's Winchester up and cocked. The woman's face broke, and tears streamed down her cheeks. "My son ran from our home because this gunman was coming after him. We don't want him in here, Sheriff! We don't want him!"

Loheed halted a few feet in front of Horse Owens and the tall cowhand named Gillman at the head of the mob of town men piling in through the doorway.

"Dammit, he should get another beatin'," Horse

growled. "That'd get him the hell out of here."

"Right. Horse's right," a second voice added. "He's got no right thinkin' he can come back and do more killin'." Others picked up the yell, joined in. A few surged forward, circling around on both sides of Slattery. "Get him! Get him while he ain't got a gun!"

Chapter Two

Shock froze Slattery, the recollection of the beating a mob like this had given him rushing to his brain. He whirled on his boot heel, pressed the flat of his back against the hard wood of the desk. Horse Owens came toward him, his immense barrel-chested body crouched, both ham-like fists doubled and ready to smash out.

"Stop this," Loheed said. He grabbed Horse's right arm. "He hasn't done any harm."

"He gunned Bol Nye in the back. And two of Jim MacCandles' cowhands." He swore, yanked his arm free. "We ain't lettin' him hunt Bromley's boy down. Not that we ain't."

Loheed moved fast around in front of the converging men, the Winchester's barrel steady in his hands.

"Back! Back! Every one of you." The muzzle swung in an arc, took in the entire mob, then centered directly into Horse's wide stomach. "Slattery's paid for that gun fight. He's served his time."

"Five years aren't enough for Nye," a close voice yelled. "We don't want Slattery here."

"He'll get out. I'll see he gets out." Loheed glanced sideways, jerked his jaw at Slattery. "Stay behind me while I walk out."

Loud talk, grumbling began, but no one moved in any nearer to the rifle. Loheed took a step forward, another. The men parted, grudgingly, opened a path.

Slattery followed the lawman, expecting someone would throw a wild swing and drive the mob onto him. Loheed halted at the screen door and shoved it open with one foot. As Slattery passed him, he grabbed the knob of the wooden front door, then back-stepped out onto the porch.

Horse's voice called after them. "Make tracks, Slattery. Next time . . ." The words were cut off as the door closed behind Loheed.

Slattery didn't slow his stride until he reached the bottom of the porch steps. He swallowed the thick, sour taste that had come with the woman's yells. The damp night wind blowing off the Platte cooled the sweat on his face and forehead. Streams of light splashed across the walks from doors and windows, and overhead, stars blinked and multiplied while the sky behind them blackened. Loheed reached his side, moved toward the black gelding tied at the hitchrail.

"Mount up," the lawman said. "Ride out. I'll get your roll and bring it to you outside town."

Slattery shook his head. "I'm not leaving, Gus. I never gunned Nye in the back. Both of Mac-Candles' gunhands were looking at me when I hit them."

"You haven't got a gun, Tom." Loheed stared into Slattery's face, saw his cold, dispassionate expression. Both men heard the hotel door open above them, and the sheriff said quietly, "I'm only

16

good for that once. I might be finished here now, Tom. But I can't go through it again."

Slattery looked at the hands that held the carbine. They were drenched with sweat, shaking. "I want to talk to Freddy Bromley. He was only fourteen when he testified. His letter said he'd thought about it all this time and he wanted to see me." He undid the halter knot, took the bridle and turned to the middle of the street. "Fischer still has those rooms over the livery. I'll take one of them."

Loheed glanced around at the porch. The men were coming out, all bunched together, all doing a lot of talking. "Listen, Tom. I'm not makin' a sermon, but I want you to listen to me. I've got to take you in if you pack a gun. There's a law here, and MacCandles knows it."

"MacCandles doesn't own the law."

"He can push you until you break it. You were let out five years early for good behavior. There's been too much talk against you. Someone'll push trouble. Once I have to take you in, MacCandles'll fix it so you'll rot in that Omaha jail."

"I won't rot in any jail," Slattery said with deceptive gentleness. "I was set up in that Nye killing." Loheed went to touch his arm and say something, but Slattery stepped away from him. "I was caged up like an animal long enough," he added, drawing a deep breath. "Sleeping on a board, eating the slop they put in front of me, never moving without a guard at my back. I took that so I could prove Pa and Joe weren't any part of the Nye murder either. I'm going to prove it,

Gus. Gun or no gun."

Loheed continued alongside him for another few yards. Then he halted. He could hear the angry conversation that went on behind him, and he dreaded going back to face it. He stood alone, worried about himself and his job, once Jim MacCandles heard what he'd done. He watched Slattery's tall form merge with the darkness of the livery work area, hunched a little, as if Tom advanced on an enemy. Loheed rubbed his hand across his mustache. He shivered involuntarily, not from the chill of the river breeze, but from the memory of the coldness in Slattery's eyes.

"Then, dammit, stay around," Horse Owens snapped to a small, skinny man near him. "He don't go now, he'll never go."

"But I got a wife and kids," the man offered weakly. "Any shootin' starts, who'll watch out for them?"

Another man close by cursed. "He wouldn't be walking now if Loheed had done his job. "You just wait 'till next election. All Slattery's got to do is get his hands on another gun."

"Hell, I know that, Horse. But I thought—"

"You don't think. You shut up."

Everyone within an arm's reach silenced, drew back a step as Owens pushed past the others on the porch and walked down into the roadway. To a man they hadn't missed the implication of the brute's sharp words, and they knew the depth of the threat there. Owens had beaten more than one man senseless right in this street for them all to see.

He'd almost killed the last homesteader who'd tried to stake out his farm north of the river.

Gillman kept his stride even with Owens'. The minute they were beyond the earshot of the crowd, he said, "Not out here, Horse. Loheed is damn fool enough to step in again."

"Look, don't tell me what to do. MacCandles said I get first crack."

"Use your thick skull then. Slattery'll keep pushin'. Give him time to get where Loheed can't cut in."

Horse's hard eyes watched Gillman. "So maybe you can. You remember MacCandles wants it this way. A man like Slattery gets killed in a street fight, there's no questions asked. You remember that."

Gillman nodded. Habitually, he hitched up his black-buckled gun rig. "I remember," he said in a calm easy voice. "And what the boss wants done just in case you miss him."

Slattery stopped his black at the wooden water trough to the left of the livery's high double doors. Inside the barn a lighted lantern hung from the rafters between the two front stalls. The scuff of a shoe on sand sounded in there, and a man holding a muzzle-loading Harper's Ferry musket walked into the lamp glare. He was old, gray-haired. The fingers that gripped the weapon were too tight, white around the knuckles.

"You don't leave your horse here, mister," he said.

"Just for the night?" asked Slattery. "He needs

watering and a good rub." He raised the bridle to the elderly hostler.

The man's head moved from side to side. "I don't own this place. I only work here. My orders are you don't leave your horse. You don't use our rooms either."

"How about some oats? Enough for tonight?"

"You get nothin', mister," the hostler said. Some of the men who had left the hotel approached on the walk. The old man glanced toward them, shifted his feet uneasily. His mouth tightened downward. "Go ahead. I need this job. You get nothin' from me."

Slattery gazed at the men, four of them shoulder to shoulder while they angled into the work area. He nodded to the old hostler, pulled on the bridle, and led the black in the direction of Center.

Once in the middle of the dirt roadway, he halted. The majority of the mob had split now. They were drifting off either toward the homes at either end of the town, or moved in one large body onto the porch of the Frontier Saloon. The bulk of the building that housed the Gunnison Restaurant loomed up opposite him, blacker than the night. Slattery drew the makings from his shirt pocket and built a cigarette. He cupped the match against the breeze. The small flame illuminated the flat planes of his face and drew a vivid outline of his head and shoulders against the dark. Inhaling deeply, he fought to calm his anger while he led the black to the restaurant hitchrail.

This anger was new, hot, one which could cause him to act on impulse, completely alien to the cold, controlled anger he'd kept locked inside him for five years. He inhaled slow and deep once more, forced a control on this new anger, subjugating it to its proper place in what he'd planned for so long. If Freddy Bromley had run from home, MacCandles had something to do with it. He knew that as surely as he knew the hate which had been built up against him was backed by MacCandles. At the rail, he tied the bridle, then flipped the cigarette butt westerly, where every window in the big new houses seemed bright with light.

Beyond the homes, the brush and timber lining the Platte was a solid thick shadow against the prairie that sloped away, rose and went down again until the starshine met the horizon. Slattery knew the area out there, the mile after mile of rolling grass spotted here and there by ranch buildings. The MacCandles spread was four miles out, built close to the river's edge. And four miles further on were the twenty acres Henry Slattery had bought for himself and his two sons. The thought of his father and brother was vivid in Slattery's mind while he went onto the restaurant porch. He made no effort to forget that or the memory of exactly how MacCandles had taken their land. That knowledge, and what a man had to do, existed of itself, was independent of any change which might come to his own will or desire.

The dining room was large and wide, with white-clothed tables arranged neatly between the door and the rear wall counter. Charlie Raine, a short, thin, take-your-time kind of a man with seedy black hair combed to cover a bald spot was alone at the grill. Slattery closed the door easily and was going past the front tables when a woman stepped out of the kitchen.

She was about thirty, a tall, slender brunette, wearing a white waitress dress. She paused in the doorway, poised and quiet, her back perfectly straight and shoulders squared while she watched Slattery sit at the counter.

Charlie Raine eyed the woman for a moment. Then a smile spread slowly over his small pale face. He took a stiff-legged step down the counter. He'd been a cowhand as a young man, but after a bronc-busting accident twelve years ago, he'd started in the restaurant business.

"Tom. Tom, boy," he said. "I'm glad to see you back."

"Thanks, Charlie."

"You must be hungry," Raine said. "You don't look like you've changed at all."

"I've changed," answered Slattery, pushing his hat back away from his forehead. Raine stared at him. There was a little gray in Slattery's black hair, parted deep on the side, and his body seemed tougher, like something durable and hard made of seasoned leather. And in the eyes, there was a change. "Well, you must be really hungry. What do you say, steak?"

"You still got those rooms upstairs?" Slattery asked. "And your barn."

"Yuh. They're used . . ." He looked away toward the kitchen as he spoke. "I lost this place to the bank. Ellen Hasslett owns it now. I only work for her."

"You can fix it up so I can use a stall."

Raine shook his head, watched Slattery's dark, hard face. "I can't do anything for you, Tom. MacCandles spread the word anyone who helped you would be out around here. Don't expect anyone to help you."

Slattery gave his head a weary shake. "Freddy Bromley was waiting to see me. Where is he, Charlie?"

"I don't know. You better order."

"Freddy said he'd either be at the hotel or he'd be in this place. Did he say anything to you?"

"No. No, he never told me nothin'." When the door swung open, Raine smiled quickly. "Steak, Tom. I'll fix you a good meal." He turned his back, busied himself at the grill. Slattery studied him for a few seconds, aware of the men who crowded into the restaurant. Horse Owens and Gillman, elbow to elbow, led the march past the tables. Horse, grinning lazily, let his glance wander to the woman. She'd stepped close to the counter, had taken a pile of plates and was arranging them in front of the stools.

"Some of you will have to use the tables," she told the crowd. "We'll serve you as soon as we can."

"We'll wait," Gillman said. "No rush, Ellie."

A snicker ran through the watchers. That and the creak of footsteps right behind him warned Slattery. Casually, hands in his pockets, Owens was sitting his weight on the next stool. The smile hadn't left his mouth, but absolutely no humor was in his voice.

23

"I'll take that steak, Charlie," he said loudly. "No bushwhacker's gonna eat before me."

Slattery gazed over his shoulder, noted the position of everyone in the room. Owens was balanced so he could slide off the stool in an instant; Gillman holding back the other men, leaving a small ring-like space open between tables and counter.

Charlie Raine stared uncertainly from Slattery to Owens. The woman said, "I don't want any trouble in here. Don't start trouble, Horse."

"Trouble? Who's startin' trouble? I just want that there steak."

Slattery glanced at the woman. She was better looking up close, her eyes very lovely, deeply brown and steady. She held herself handsomely, her chin raised, back straight, and both hands resting on the checkered oilcloth of the counter. "Give him the steak," he said to her quietly. "I'll wait."

"Yellow, too," Owens snarled. "I figured that, the way you shot an old man in the back."

"You've got your steak," Slattery said. "Let it go at that."

"The hell, I'll let it go. I want that stool, yellow. That's the stool I always take. Charlie, ain't that the stool I always take?"

Charlie had backed limpingly away from the grill, had found a rag and was cleaning the spotless surface of the far end of the counter. As if he'd been slapped in the face, he nodded quickly.

"See, that's my stool," Owens repeated, still grinning.

24

"Horse," Slattery said tiredly, "isn't the steak enough?"

"I get that stool!"

The two voices, one loud and grating, the other quiet, were the only sounds in the room. Slattery watched the men, thrilled and expectant. The woman, white-faced, had started to pick up the plates again. "I don't want trouble," she said fearfully. "I can't afford to have you wreck my dining room."

"You weren't here when this bushwhacker killed old Bol Nye," Owens said. "Rotten stinkin' . . . I won't eat with you, Slattery."

Someone in the crowd chuckled at the louder, nastier words. It would get worse, Slattery knew. He kept a tight grip on his temper, knowing a fight would smash and wreck everything in the restaurant. The few dollars he had wouldn't pay even a slight percentage of the damage. He'd be locked up in Loheed's jail, waiting for a state guard to come out and take him back to Omaha.

Slattery nodded to the woman and slid off the stool. "Obliged, Miss," he said. "You better serve these people first." He moved around the close tables, headed for the door.

The shocked men at the front opened a way, and he stepped past them quickly. The expectant stares were gone, replaced by frowns and hateful glares. A voice cursed, "Damned coward!" Many more insults followed him to the door.

Slattery hadn't closed the door before he caught Owen's filthy swearing and the heavy footfall of his hobnailed boots behind him. He stepped onto the porch. A crowd had formed below in the street. He could even make out the faces of women and children in the lamplight of the walks. His boot touched the boards of the top step when his arm was grabbed from behind and he was jerked around.

"I don't want this," Slattery said. "I left the restaurant so it wouldn't start."

"Either fight or get out of town," Owens yelled into his face. He was fairly shaking with rage, his barrel-like chest bare inches from Slattery's shoulder. A woman called, "Get the sheriff! Horse will kill him!"

"Let him. Let him," a man said. "It's what he's got comin'! Let him!"

Horse Owens crowded Slattery, forcing him toward the street. Five years, Slattery thought, and I didn't even get as far as facing MacCandles. He turned away, moved with his back to Owens, letting the people see he was trying even now to stop this. Inside, he felt his own hate unloosen, his pulse quicken, and he let his mounting cold fury take hold. He was ready and he waited for Owens to grab him, his fists doubled, his mind sharp and deadly calm.

Chapter Three

The crowd split, fanned out wide in front of him. Owens' fist grabbed Slattery's shoulder. He winced as the huge man shoved him hard from the rear, throwing him headlong into the dirt.

Slattery pushed himself up, still tried to back away. His immense head bobbing up and down, half-smiling in enjoyment, Horse Owens kicked out with his hobnailed boot. The toe grazed Slattery's left shoulder and he stumbled to that side as if he'd been thrown off balance.

Owens laughed wildly. His big right fist came up, poised. With his left he seized Slattery's arm and began to swing him around in order to smash his face.

Slattery whirled in a complete turn, bringing his elbow back violently into the middle of Owens' stomach. The suddenness and force of the blow startled Owens, doubling him over. Grunting, he straightened almost instantly and moved in, completely confident, sure he'd finish off Slattery fast.

Slattery edged to the left, realizing he couldn't stand toe-to-toe and slug it out with this bulldog type of fighter. He had to use the giant's over-confidence, or his brute strength and weight would gradually wear him down. He halted momentarily, feinted to draw Owens in.

Owens took the bait. He charged forward, throwing his powerful right in a vicious roundhouse. Slattery weaved away and the blow missed by mere inches. The quick movement threw Owens off balance, giving Slattery the advantage he wanted.

He charged, bringing both fists up as though he intended to center his attack on Owens' face. The instant Owens' guard raised, Slattery smashed solid lefts and rights into his stomach. His third blow sunk in a little, the fourth went deeper. Owens cursed in confused rage. He brought one arm down to cover his middle, swung out with the other to encircle Slattery's shoulders and hold him close.

Slattery jerked his body away. The huge man floundered ahead clumsily, grabbed only air. Slattery's right rose, opened while it chopped down in a long arc, striking like an axe against the jugular vein of the thick neck. At the tremendous impact, Owens bellowed, straightened.

Slattery side-stepped, brought the right around again. The solid flat of his hand slashed into the big, reddened face, hit the bridge of the nose. The bone snapped, flattened, gushed blood.

Owens screamed in pain and jerked his head back. Then, by sheer instinct he lunged forward again. Slattery pounded him, two, three times in the stomach. The muscles there had no rigidity now. Owens rocked on his feet, tried to stay erect.

Slattery pressed in, head jammed against the heaving chest. He swung from the waist. The long uppercut struck solidly into the throat just below the jawbone, hitting with a loud snapping, whipcrack noise.

Owens spun around and dropped to the ground. He lay there, choking, coughing into the dust as he fought to breathe, his bloody nose dripping blobs of wet dirt. He began to push himself up, but after a single weak, hopeless try, he dropped flat again and used all his remaining strength to squeeze air into his lungs.

Slattery straightened, his chest rising and falling rapidly. For a moment there was no sound, the onlookers gaped in amazed disbelief. Only Gillman moved. One hand hanging loose beside his gun, he stepped out into the open beside Owens and bent to help the big man stand. Then muttering broke out, soft, guarded words that gradually grew louder. Slattery read the hate-filled looks, wondered how many others who felt the same as Owens would come after him now.

The solid steel barrel of a gun jammed into Slattery's back. He heard Gus Loheed's voice close to his ear.

"This is the way you want it, you'll get it." The Colt waved across the street. "Over to the jail, Slattery."

Slattery said, "Gus, I didn't want this. I tried to keep it from happening."

The six-gun waved again. "You knew what'd happen."

"He wasn't to blame for that fight, Sheriff," Ellen Hasslett said coming down the steps of her restaurant. "He did try to keep from fighting. I saw the whole thing."

"It was up to him to make sure he kept out of a

fight, Ellen."

"He had no choice, Sheriff. He walked out here, but Owens followed him and attacked him. You can't arrest him for defending himself."

"That don't matter," a man near Loheed said. "He can't find a place to stay. I don't want him walkin' the streets while I'm asleep."

"Me either," a second added. "Keep him in jail, Gus. 'Till they come after him from Omaha."

Ellen stared around at the circle of faces as if she didn't understand. Quickly, her eyes flared. "He has a room if he wants one," she said. "Over my restaurant. He can use my barn for his horse."

Slattery said, "Look, Miss. You don't know what you're . . ."

"I know. I know you didn't start any trouble here. I know this is so unfair I think it's terrible." She turned to Loheed. "Sheriff?"

Loheed rubbed his jaw, glanced around. Gillman had pulled Owens to his feet. The huge man stood awkwardly, massaging his neck with both hands. "He was lucky," he said in a hoarse voice. "I'll kill him." He spat a mouthful of blood, watched Slattery hatefully.

"You'll do nothing," Loheed told him. "This ends right here. Gillman, get him over to Doc's so's he can fix that nose." And to Slattery, "You can use the room tonight. But you ride out tomorrow. That straight?"

"Gus, I didn't shoot Nye. I don't want to mix a woman in this."

"Out tomorrow," the lawman repeated. "Get up

in that room. Now." His eyes flicked around the circle of bystanders. Slattery followed his gaze, seeing how all the men pressed together, their expressions hard and watchful. It would take only one word, one wrong move for them to turn into a mob.

Ellen Hasslett started up the stairs.

"I'll be in to see you tomorrow," Slattery said to the sheriff. And he walked up onto the restaurant porch with the woman.

Chapter Four

The staircase to the second floor was inside the kitchen. Ellen Hasslett hesitated to light a lantern before she reached the swinging doors. She glanced at Charlie Raine. "Take Mr. Slattery's steak up to him," she told the old cook. "And some coffee."

"Sure. I'll bring it up now, Ellie."

She led the way through an immaculately clean kitchen where big pots and pans and boilers, the stove, the cutlery and stacks of dishes, gleamed in the bright lamplight. At the top of the stairs she paused long enough to insert the key in the door lock.

Slattery said, "Look, I'll go out back to the barn. You've done enough helping me in front of all those people."

Ellen dismissed that with a defiant toss of her head. "I didn't do that just for you. I'm so sick of this town and the way people act." She stepped inside. The room looked bare, with only an iron-posted bed, a single cane-backed chair and a small bureau with an attached mirror shoved into one corner. The window had white curtains and a drawn green shade. She shook her head. "It isn't much, but it's better than a jail cell."

"Well, I'm very satisfied. This is better than I'd get at the hotel. This is really decent of you."

She stared at him and smiled, and the smile made her pretty face suddenly younger, more feminine and friendly. "I'll get you sheets and some blankets and towels so you can wash. You've ridden such a long way."

"You know where I've been," he said quietly.

"All about it. You'd think from the talk that has been spread about you the last month, you'd be coming into town shooting. Not turning your back on that bully like you did down there." Footsteps approached on the stairs, and she gazed at Charlie Raine, coming through the doorway carrying a tray of food. "Just put it on the bureau," she told him.

She left and Raine limped across the room to the bureau. He pushed the lantern aside, set the tray on the top.

"I cooked up another steak fast," he said, grinning. "If it's too rare, Tom, I'll do it some more." He lifted the chair, moved it to the bureau, then stepped back, still grinning uneasily.

"Thanks, Charlie." He slipped his coat off and dropped it over the bedpost. "Charlie, Freddy Bromley used to run errands for you. Did he hang around here much?"

"Yuh." He glanced at the shaded window, cocked his head a little toward the doorway. "He's a good kid, Tom. If he said anything wrong at the trial, he was just a kid."

"He was fourteen then. He's nineteen now. That's old enough to answer questions like a man."

Raine rubbed his hands together, nervous and uncertain. "I didn't figure you'd go after him. I didn't, Tom."

"I'm not after him. He wrote me. He said he wanted to talk to me. I want to talk to him. That's all."

"Only talk." Raine wet his thin lips and looked away toward the stairs. "I'm not sure. Maybe he'll come back."

"He said he might be in the restaurant if he wasn't home. Why, Charlie?"

"I don't know. The young folks come in here some nights for a bite. They all come in." He turned toward the door, but Slattery grabbed his arm. "Did he mention the letter to you, Charlie. He was closer to you than he was to his own father."

"Let go my arm."

"I'm not after the kid to hurt him. Someone else has more reason to hurt him than me. He saw the one who shot Nye run away past the hotel. He didn't see me." He dropped Raine's arm.

Raine shook his head. "If only you hadn't threatened to kill MacCandles at the trial."

"I was hot-headed. I had nothing but ten years of jail ahead of me because of MacCandles. I've learned something about shooting off my mouth since then. Did Freddy say anything to you?"

Raine rubbed one hand over his bony jaw. "He started to Tuesday night. But the Ellsons came in and he didn't finish."

"Matt Ellson worked for MacCandles. Does he still?"

"Yes. Both him and his kid brother. Freddy's been hangin' with them lately."

"And he was with them the night he left?"

Raine nodded. "They left here for the Frontier. 'Bout nine o'clock."

Slattery stared at him a few moments, his face drawn and hard. Matt Ellson had been one of the witnesses who'd sworn he'd seen Slattery's father and brother go out the back door of Bromley's Hotel before Bol Nye was murdered. Slattery stepped to the window, drew aside the shade. The long, half-frosted glass window of the Frontier Saloon was brightly lit, and the same lamplight threw streaks of yellow onto the porch above and below the batwings. He could hear the tinkle of a piano coming from there, could see that a lot of men had stayed on inside, and in the general store and the barber shop. The wind was blowing harder now; it whisked dust up in small waves along Center, which was darkly shadowed in the half hour before the moon rises.

It wasn't shadowed enough for him to miss the form of a man standing at the hitchrail of the gunsmith's. Gillman had stationed himself out far enough for everyone to see him. He made no effort to conceal the fact that he was watching the restaurant. The lighted cigarette in his mouth showed that.

Slattery dropped the shade into place. "All right, Charlie," he said. "I appreciate your telling me. I just wish you'd told me earlier."

"I wasn't sure," Raine answered, a small flush of self-anger showing under his eyes. "They've all been hangin' out at MacCandles' ranch. Freddy's out there as much as anyone."

"Will you feed my horse and rub him down?"

Slattery said, walking to the bureau. "And saddle him again when he's rested?"

"Sure. Sure, I'll be glad to." He twisted his pale, bony hands together. The worry was gone from his face, replaced by a smile, trying to coax understanding into Slattery's bitter eyes. "You can see I couldn't know, Tom. You see why I wasn't positive? You see how it was, don't you?"

Slattery pulled out the chair to sit. Ellen came into the room, her arms loaded with sheets, blankets and towels. Slattery nodded to Raine. "Sure, Charlie. Don't worry about it."

"I'll take care of his horse," Charlie said to Ellen. "All right?"

"Go ahead. There are no customers down there. I'll hear if anyone comes in."

She walked to the bed and set down the linens. She remained silent while Slattery started to eat. In the quiet she made the bed. Slattery ate slowly, without talking, yet he followed every movement she made.

Finally, he said, "I certainly needed that. I'd forgotten what real home cooking was like."

She didn't look around, but fluffed the pillow before she put it into the pillowcase. "This bed is more comfortable than it looks. You should get a good night's rest."

"I may go out for a little while. I won't wake you."

"I don't sleep here, Mr. Slattery. My house is up at the west end." She turned to face him down over the top of the pillowcase. When she spoke her voice was different. She was no longer the woman

36

who'd helped him, but a quiet-spoken friend.

"Will you take advice, Mr. Slattery?"

"Depends, Miss Hasslett."

"Ellen," she said. "I hope you'll take mine. I've never seen such hate built up for a man as I've seen this last month. The people here are actually frightened to death of you. They've talked of nothing else but having you arrested again so you'd be sent to jail for life. If I were you, I'd leave Gunnison tomorrow morning for good."

"I can't, Ellen."

"You can. You're a free man now. Forget what's happened and go somewhere else and make a life for yourself. This town or its people aren't worth going back to prison for."

"You don't mean that."

She raised an eyebrow, watched him, not answering.

"You can see what the people are like," he said, "but you stay yourself. There must be some reason."

Ellen laid the pillow at the head of the bed, smoothed out the cloth. "I bought this restaurant four years ago, before I knew what it was really like. I believed what I'd read about the opportunities in the west."

"You didn't have to stay."

"I had hopes, Tom," she said, and she walked closer to his chair. She raised a hand so he wouldn't answer. "My father left me enough to get along on when he died. I thought I could make a go . . ." She shook her head. "I didn't know how a town could be run by one man, and how you can

37

get into such a hole that you have to stick, even when you hate to so much you can't stand it."

"MacCandles?"

"Yes. He owns these people," she said frowning at the window. "He owns every inch of land north of the river."

"I know."

"You don't know about the people. You can't know. You have to live here to see it. Every business, every store, even the houses depend on the money the MacCandles ranch and cowhands spend here. I couldn't even sell out and get my money back unless I dealt with Mr. James Mac-Candles." She brushed her hands tensely down the sides of her dress. "There are too many ways that MacCandles tries to deal with you. I've learned that."

"I can understand how he'd try," Slattery said. He'd noted how the touching of her clothing had outlined the clean curve of her hips and the neat swell below the bosom of her dress. The greed MacCandles had shown in his ruthless fight to control a cattle empire had to have a further outlet, and Ellen's loveliness would be natural game for him.

Ellen said, "You won't change your mind about leaving tonight?"

"I know what I have to do, Ellen."

She nodded slowly. "I'll have Charlie leave a key with your roll. I have a revolver downstairs—it's an old one and there are only three bullets in it. But I'll give it to Charlie for you."

"I'll take it. Thanks. For everything."

She looked at him for another few seconds, then without saying anything more she turned and walked out of the room.

Slattery set the knife and fork down on the plate and stood. He took a deep breath, listening to her soft footsteps recede along the stairs. Such a beautiful woman, alone actually, and as much of a prisoner here as he'd been in jail. He moved to the window, inched the shade from the glass. Gillman was still at the post, still smoking. Around his boots dirt blew up in the wind, and beyond him the same dust made small gritty halos on porches wherever an outside lamp swung.

Slattery returned to the bureau. He turned up the lamp wick, giving the room a whiter, brighter light. For the next ten minutes he moved around, throwing his shadow across the shade often so there would be no doubt in Gillman's mind he was still in the room. Then, he picked up his coat and put it on while he stepped through the doorway onto the stairs.

Charlie Raine was worried and afraid. Since he'd led Slattery's black around behind the restaurant, he'd kept his eyes and ears open, expecting anything to happen. He hadn't wanted one bit of this trouble. He'd had enough after Slattery's trial because he'd refused to take part in the beating the mob had given Tom the night of the Nye killing. All he could do was stand by and watch while the town men, led by MacCandles' cowhands, grabbed him from Gus Loheed and beat him until he couldn't walk. Charlie had felt MacCandles' long arm soon enough. Customers had dropped off gradually. He'd had to borrow more and more money, and he'd finally folded.

Now, listening for every sound that came—animals moving about on the flat or in the brush along the river, the piano music and talk that was carried down the alley every so often by the wind—he feared what might happen to him. There were so many men out to get Slattery. All they'd have to do was learn he'd grained and rubbed down the black, and had put its saddle on again. And about the old Starr .45 Ellen had given him to hold for Slattery. It wouldn't be just his way of making a living he'd lose. He couldn't take a beating with his game leg, not the kind they'd given Slattery.

Raine swung around at the sound of a door closing, stared fearfully past the lantern he'd hung between the two front stalls. The small yard was quiet, just beginning to lighten at the first sign of the moon. He slapped the gelding on the rump, made him go into the left stall. Then he slipped into the thick black shadows near the rear door of the building, his stiff-legged backward limp shuffling in an uneven pattern.

Slattery appeared, his long body silhouetted in the yellow lamplight. He walked directly to the stall, stood for a moment looking around.

Raine moved out from behind the ladder that led to the hay mow. "He's all set to go," he said. He bent over, felt through the hay at the corner of the stall until he found the Starr revolver he'd hidden. "Ellie told me to give you this."

Slattery took the weapon. "I appreciate this, Charlie." He revolved the drum, checked the load.

Raine nodded, peered out through the doorway. The roof tops toward the east seemed lighter. In another few minutes the moon would be up and the prairie would be brilliantly lit, giving Slattery less chance of riding out unseen. He shivered suddenly, partly at the thought of what could be waiting out there, mainly for his own fear.

"I won't be here when you get back," he said. "I'm usin' Upjohn's house. You'll have to see to him yourself."

"I will. Thanks, Charlie." Slattery took the bridle and led the black out through the rear door.

Charlie Raine stood without moving until the sound of the horse's hoofs died. He pushed onto his tiptoes, reached up to turn down the lamp. He didn't hear a footstep behind him, saw only the shadow of a man's tall shape at his side, then move past him.

Nate Gillman halted at the rear door, listened. His lean, tight-skinned face was completely blank when he looked around at Charlie.

"He have a gun?" he said.

"Loheed took his gun. His rifle too."

"You or that woman in there could've gotten one to him." The eyes in the cowhand's calm face had narrowed.

"He's got an old Starr. He might be leavin' for good."

"He's leavin' all right." Gillman's eyes had narrowed into slits. "You tell nobody I was in here. Get that!"

"I get it . . . yes."

The tall cowhand stepped forward and walked fast to the front door. He cut left hurriedly, and disappeared into the black shadows of the yard.

Chapter Five

Close to the river the windows of the houses were closed and shutters were drawn against the damp breeze, but Slattery still held the gelding down to a slow walk. The very silence of the trees and brush was a threat in itself, as though the extreme quiet concealed a trap, and he couldn't chance being caught out here. He kept his right hand on the butt of the Starr revolver. With the sight jammed below his waistband, it might catch if he had to draw fast. He had two names to go on: Matt and Billy Ellson. Matt had been in town the night Bol Nye was killed. He'd been one of MacCandles' guns right from the start, but young Billy was another matter.

Slattery remembered him as a boy just a couple years older than Freddy Bromley, weak and mouthy about his brother's working for Mac-Candles. Now he was twenty-one or two, hanging around with Freddy for a reason. He could be an opening in this, Slattery thought coldly. He'd see. But for the present, his mind stayed on the timber, his eyes probing the blackness that lay behind each clump of willows, along the sandbars, and beyond in the lighter grayishness of the flat.

He hadn't stopped at the tree-shaded acre of land the citizens of Gunnison used as a cemetery. He'd simply passed close enough to the rear

43

cottonwoods to stare past the neat lines of dark gravestones at the barren sandy corner where his father and brother were buried. He'd thought often enough in jail that there had been a certain kindness to his mother's dying in that bad Texas winter of sixty-eight. She hadn't had to watch her husband and sons lose the ranch to the carpetbaggers, and then the two of them shot down in a back alley for something they hadn't done. About two things he'd never change: he'd clear the Slattery name here, and Joe and their father would be moved from that pauper's plot.

The moon was up before he'd gone two miles. The darkness faded, the trees and prairie becoming gradually outlined against the hazy horizon. The sandbars and rocks took on a whitish shine, as though they'd suddenly risen wet and gleaming out of the black water. The stars began to brighten, clear flakes of light in the bluish sky. A single coyote howled from the prairie far beyond the high south bank. Its rising, drawn-out wail broke at the end in a shower of yelps that echoed eerily among the trees.

After almost an hour he struck the small stream that cut into the Platte from the upper quarter of the MacCandles range. He spoke softly to the gelding and turned him down the bank, letting him pick his own way through the sluggish channel. The horse stopped to drink. Slattery sat his saddle easily, his bandana pulled up to his eyes to hold off the mosquitoes and fireflies. He was rubbing the animal's neck, his eyes on the small dots of light far ahead, almost hidden by the endless swells of tall grass, when the black lifted its head, shaking the last of the water from its mouth.

The gelding's neck muscles were hard as wood. The animal watched the junction of the river and stream. Slattery listened, but he could hear nothing. He wasn't fooled, though. The black had caught a sound from that direction.

Abruptly, Slattery kneed the horse forward, up the bank and into the willow thicket. In the same motion, he eased the .45 from his waistband.

Seconds dragged past, then he heard the rustle of the brush opposite him.

The horse and rider appeared, black shapes at first, slowly moved down the bank into the stream.

Slattery waited until the rider began to turn his mount up the bank. He kneed the black out of the willows. He held the Starr centered on Gillman's head.

Gillman reined in, let his right hand drop. Slattery's hard voice said, "Go ahead. Give me a reason."

"What in hell you pullin'?" Both hands raised above the pommel, rested there.

"You're just riding back to your ranch, I know," Slattery said. "Reach across with your left and drop the six-gun."

Gillman stared down at the water.

"I want to hear it splash," Slattery told him. He waited, and Gillman slid the weapon out and let it drop. When it struck the water, Slattery nodded. "Now the carbine."

Gillman started to say something, but, watching Slattery's face, he remained quiet. He wiped his mouth with the sleeve of his shirt, slipped his Spencer rifle from its scabbard. Even in the hazy light, Slattery could read the intense hate in his blank expression.

Gillman watched the water cover the long steel barrel. His gaze shifted to Slattery. "Okay, what do we do?"

"We go to MacCandles' place together." A slight shift of his wrist and the black swung to the left. "I'll follow you."

Gillman leaned forward. "I figure you owe me the cost of both those guns."

"Get it from MacCandles. He got our spread for a hundredth of what it was worth."

Gillman allowed him a hard grin. He spurred his mount, pushed up the bank and into the brush ahead of Slattery. They rode in silence. Soon, they cut into a river trail that wound across the flat and merged with a well-worn wagon road leading to the sprawling ranch house and buildings of the Circle M. They were half a mile from the gate when Slattery learned the reason for all the lights which showed in the windows. The strains of "Turkey in the Straw" and the sounds of people laughing came softly through the quiet of the night.

Men and women were out on the long veranda that ran the length of the house front. Slattery's eyes didn't leave the growth of cottonwoods and alders which grew behind the bunkhouse. If Mac-Candles had anyone watching, they'd either be there or among the buggies, wagons and horses lined up in the broad tree-shaded yard. Once past the first lighted window, he returned the .45 to his waistband and drew his coat front over the handle. He pulled up even with Gillman, and together they rode directly to the stairs of the veranda.

"You go in and tell MacCandles I want to talk to Freddy Bromley," Slattery said.

"The Bromley kid isn't here. Mr. MacCandles is throwing this shindig for some of his friends. He's got no reason to have that kid out here."

"Tell MacCandles what I said."

Gillman didn't move his head. The people on the porch had seen their approach and three or four of the men drifted away from their wives to the top step. Gillman eyed them. He was bent forward in the saddle, both hands gripping the horn. He grinned at Slattery. "Okay, I'll get Mr. Mac-Candles."

He'd straightened in the saddle, one boot out of the stirrup. The boot shot back, jabbed the spur rowels deep into his mare's side, making it lunge forward. Watching for something like that, Slattery pulled the black away. One outstretched hand locked on Gillman's shoulder. Gillman tried to keep his balance, but Slattery jerked him sideways and threw him violently to the ground.

Talk erupted among the people on the porch. Slattery halted his horse, sat straight looking down at Gillman. "Freddy Bromley's the one I'd like to talk to. Tell your boss."

Dazed from the fall, Gillman fought to get to his feet. Blood oozed from his nose and one corner of his mouth. "Damn you," he threatened, "I'll get . . ."

"That's enough, Nate!"

The call was loud, demanding. Gillman stopped where he was.

Jim MacCandles walked past the men and halted at the edge of the porch. He was a big man in his middle forties, with the lean, disciplined body of a working rancher. He wore an expensive gray suit that broke correctly over his polished shoes. The young woman who'd come out with him was a handsome brunette, tall and finely shaped in her low-cut blue gown. MacCandles touched her arm lightly, and she waited with the others while the rancher descended the stairs.

There was nothing to be learned from Mac Candles' features, which were tanned and leather hard, nor from his dark eyes, tight and sharp beneath thick black eyebrows. "Well, what do you want, Slattery?" he asked.

"Watch him, Mr. MacCandles," Gillman warned. "He's packin' a gun."

MacCandles halted and stood leisurely, not paying attention to Gillman's words. Slattery didn't know whether he'd seen him throw Gillman or not. MacCandles was cold and controlled. Slattery had never been able to guess accurately about anything connected to Jim MacCandles. If he'd been able to, he never would've walked into the trap he knew this man had set up five years ago.

"I want to talk to Freddy Bromley," Slattery said quietly. "I was told he came out here with the Ellson brothers."

"He never heard that," Gillman said, wiping blood from his nose. "Mr. MacCandles, let me

48

handle this."

"Keep out of this," Jim MacCandles snapped. He'd been aware of the conversation which went on behind him, and that his sharp words had also silenced whatever was being said. He nodded to Slattery. His voice was very calm, easy. "Freddy was out here yesterday. But he left about an hour before sundown."

"How about the Ellsons?"

A man spoke up on the porch. "You ain't obliged to listen to him, Jim. There's enough of us to ride him out of here." Other voices began to echo the statement.

MacCandles raised one hand and the talk died. He looked at Gillman. "Go down to the bunkhouse and get the Ellsons."

Gillman stared at the rancher.

"Go ahead," MacCandles repeated. "Tell them to come out here. Right now."

Gillman started across the moonlit yard toward the bunkhouse, and MacCandles glanced around at the porch. "You folks go back in and dance. This has nothing to do with you."

"We'll stay, Jim."

"Yeah, you haven't got a gun, but some of us have."

MacCandles turned again to Slattery. "You can ask anything you want. Just don't go trying to carry out those threats you made in court."

"You figured I'd be back, MacCandles."

"I'd hoped you wouldn't. I offered you Slatterys a fair price for your land. The idea I was trying to take over every ranch in the territory is ridiculous. Every man here owns his own land, and you can see they're my friends."

Slattery's gaze had taken in the watchers. Those he recognized all had small spreads on the south side of the Platte. Their land had never interested MacCandles. It wasn't rich soil like this side of the river, but was so windblown and dry, its sand was splotched with patches of alkali and grew only spotty grass that made running cows beyond river drinking distance almost impossible. He was going to give an answer, but the door of the bunkhouse had swung out and Gillman and Matt and Billy Ellson were walking toward him.

Both Ellsons were stubby and wirey. Billy hung a step behind his older brother. He grinned confidently at MacCandles when they reached him. "Yes, sir, Mr. MacCandles?" he said.

MacCandles didn't return the smile. "Tom Slattery is looking for young Bromley. He was with you here yesterday."

"He's been with you two a lot lately," Slattery told them. "That right?"

Matt Ellson's square jaw stiffened. His stare locked with Slattery's. "Listen," he said. "Mr. MacCandles says I tell the truth. That don't mean I take any of your guff."

Slattery nodded patiently.

Jim MacCandles said, "Answer any questions he asks, Matt. Slattery, I have guests, and I'm getting a little sick of this."

"Where's Freddy now?" Slattery said to the Ellsons.

Matt glanced at his younger brother. Billy

50

shrugged. "How should we know? He rode out with us from town yesterday. We sat 'round in the bunkhouse 'till four. No, five. 'Cause Cookie asked him to stay for grub, but he said he wanted to get back home. He didn't get home, it's got nothin' to do with us."

"That's all."

"He rode off," Matt said. "We don't know nothin' else." He pursed his lips while he stared up at Slattery. "Except that he was scared stiff of you. He knew you were comin' back. He was only a kid when you threatened him."

Whispers started. Slattery shook his head. "He isn't down in that bunkhouse now? Or in the barn?"

Matt Ellson's deep-set eyes hardened. "You asked what we know. We told you, mister."

"You can search the bunkhouse and barn," MacCandles said to Slattery. "After you're satisfied, get off my land."

"How about the house?" Slattery's eyes raised at the shocked flutter of talk that brought.

"Get him out of here," a man snapped. "You've gone along with him, Jim, and what good did it do you?"

MacCandles' hand raised. He smiled at the speaker. "No," he said, matter-of-factly, "this man accused me of being behind the shooting of his father and brother. He killed two of my own hired hands in a gunfight. He'll be gone, but after he is, I don't want one bit of doubt left in anyone's mind." The smile vanished as he spoke to Slattery. "You don't step one foot into my home. These

51

people have been here all evening and they've been in every room. If any one of them wants, he can look through the entire house for you. But you don't step one foot inside."

A silence fell, a taut, heavy quiet that stretched out while the men on the porch edged closer to the stairs. A warning stirred in Slattery, making him see the threat in their deliberate manner, and in Jim MacCandles' hard, watchful eyes. In the end, it was MacCandles who broke the silence.

"Either search the barn and bunkhouse or ride out."

"I don't figure the boy's here," Slattery said flatly. "But I'll talk to him."

MacCandles nodded. "You decide. Once you ride off my land, you don't come back. I don't intend to fool with you. Understand that?"

"I've understood that for five years, Mac-Candles." Slattery swung the black and rode slowly across the yard.

MacCandles turned around, looked seriously at the men and women on the porch. "Go back inside," he said. "Please. This is over now." He smiled at the brunette. "Barbara, George Harris will take you in. I'll only be a few minutes."

"Of course, Jim," the woman answered. She smiled at the man who'd taken her arm and moved toward the front doorway.

MacCandles stepped away from the porch to the center of the yard. Slattery was already out of sight in the thick moon-thrown shadows of the timber behind the bunkhouse.

Nate Gillman said, "He looked through the

windows when he went by, Mr. MacCandles. He might've seen . . ."

"Shut up," MacCandles snapped, loud and cold. "You've done enough tonight." He stood motionless for several seconds, still watching the flat.

Jim MacCandles' manner was making Gillman tense. He felt at the tender skin of his scraped cheek. "He came up on me in the dark," he offered carefully. "He won't get that chance again."

Jim MacCandles stared at him. "No. Not you. He's got absolutely nothing to go on or he would've looked. With an army here, that man would've looked. Will Gruber rode out after the fight Slattery had with Owens." He shifted his stare to Matt Ellson. "You get into town ahead of him. Circle wide out on the flat so he won't hear you. Tell Horse I'll double the money if he gets Slattery. He's got a reason. He can do it any way he wants."

"Dang right," Matt Ellson said grinning broadly. He slapped his gunless hip, began to head for the bunkhouse.

"No, you don't wear a gun," MacCandles said. "You stay in only long enough to tell Horse. Whatever happens it has nothing to do with this ranch. Not with any of us. You just tell Horse he'll get paid, but he has to finish Slattery strictly on his own."

Chapter Six

Slattery rode eastward at a steady pace, following the right bank of the Platte until he reached the junction of the Circle M stream and the river. There he pulled the gelding into the cover of some scrub willows and swung around in the saddle. The floodlight glare of the almost-full moon overpowered the stars, giving the vast grassy plain a whitish shine. The line of cottonwoods and alders behind him stood like silent shadowed sentinels guarding the glassy blackness of the water. Only the steady low rustle of the wind through the leaves came to him, the single sound accenting the irony of the night's stillness, masking the hate he'd left behind him. Despite the humming mosquitoes and fireflies which kept after him, he sat for another long minute without a movement, straining to catch any noise on his backtrail.

Shortly, he kneed the horse down onto a sandbar and across to the opposite bank. By crossing this way he'd hear anyone who attempted to come up on him. He didn't try to fool himself. Riding out here to face MacCandles directly had been a mistake. He hadn't learned one new fact, and MacCandles had used the entire incident to build more of a backing for himself. Slattery rode slowly, thinking, mulling over each word of the talk which had gone on; he tried to recall every expression on every face. His mind stuck on the way MacCandles had shifted every question about Freddy Bromley from himself, how he'd separated himself from anything to do with the boy.

The Ellsons had been waiting for him all along. They'd had their answers ready, and it would have been useless to push the other ranchers by looking in any of the Circle M ranch buildings. He wondered now if he'd ever see Freddy Bromley, or if anyone would ever see him again.

The chilly breeze brought him snatches of town noises while he was still a quarter-mile away. The tinkle of the saloon piano, the loud slam of a door, the bark of a dog. They were all common sounds, but in the quiet of the brush and the cool light of the moon, they reminded him he couldn't be too cautious when he was back among the people.

Once he recrossed the river, he kept to the brush until he could angle past only a few of the backyards to the restaurant barn. He was thirty feet from the building when the barn door opened, showing a wide streak of lamplight. A man stepped outside. His body was etched vaguely for only a fraction of a moment, making it impossible for Slattery to recognize him.

Slattery jerked the Starr .45, felt it snag on the cloth of his trousers as he swung out of the saddle.

He was on the ground now, crouched like a cat, revolver in hand, moving away from the gelding.

"Tom. That you, Tom?" said Charlie Raine's voice.

"Yes."

Raine's small thin form limped close to him. "Ellie had me wait for you." His glance was on the gun. "Freddy Bromley's father has been inside waitin' for you."

"How long?"

" 'Bout a half hour. He's the only one who's come in tonight, so don't worry. No one else knows you've been out. I'll take your horse."

Slattery handed the old cook the revolver and went into the barn. Through the rear window of the restaurant, he could see Ellen Hasslett had waited in the kitchen for him. She met him when he opened the door. Her pretty face was worried, her steady brown eyes bright as they looked him up and down.

"You gave the gun to Charlie," she said. "Good. I don't know what Mr. Bromley wants. He wouldn't tell me."

"Charlie says you haven't had any customers all night. I'll move out after I talk to him."

"No, don't do that." She was near him, so close her white dress brushed him. "There isn't any place you can go," she said evenly, but a trace of color had come into her cheeks. "I don't care about this restaurant." She shook her head quickly. "Not after the way people have acted tonight. I don't want to live like this."

"Well, I don't know," he said slowly. "We'll see."

He went to step away and she asked. "Everything went all right at MacCandles' ranch? You saw the Bromley boy?"

"Freddy wasn't there. MacCandles was throwing

a party, and someone's face would've showed it if they knew where he was. If the kid's hiding somewhere, I can't go asking to look through every ranch around here."

"I'm sorry, Tom," she said. The color had receded from her cheeks. She watched him. "Why don't you give this up? The town isn't worth it. It isn't, Tom."

Slattery looked at her in silence. He shook his head, then pushed through the swinging doors.

Martin Bromley sat at one of the window tables. He stood the instant he saw Slattery. His graying head held stiffly, his deep-lined face watched the double doors as though he expected someone else would enter behind Slattery.

"You want to talk to me, Mr. Bromley?"

"You've been out of town. They told me you were sleeping upstairs, but I know you were away from town."

"I rode out to MacCandles' place to talk to your son." The elderly man rubbed one hand across his jaw tiredly, said. "You didn't make him come back with you?"

"He wasn't out there, Mr. Bromley."

Bromley stared at him, surprised and just as quickly the expression vanished, hidden behind an unsure calmness. "You wouldn't have learned anything from him. You wouldn't have. That letter he wrote—he was just a boy when he was on the witness stand. He said only what he thought was right. Please don't hold it against him."

"Do you know what he wanted to talk to me about?"

Bromley's head shook. "He didn't have anything to tell you. He was afraid of you. He's remembered every day since you've been away what you threatened."

"I threatened MacCandles. Only MacCandles. If the boy told the truth, he had no reason to worry. Or to run away."

"But he believed you meant him. He—"

"Why?"

Bromley's face began to break, and he bit down on his lower lip. "He was only a boy. He'd naturally be afraid. After the way you killed two of the MacCandles cowhands. I know it's been hard on you, but in the name of— Please, leave here. We have money. We'll help you get started again."

Slattery nodded toward the front door. "You'd better go, Mr. Bromley. I don't want your money. I'm not going to harm your son."

Bromley raised one hand, tentatively, as if he meant to touch Slattery's arm. Then he let it fall to his side, "I didn't want the offer to sound like that. I just want my son alive and well."

"That's what I want too," Slattery said. He walked toward the door with the old hotel owner. "You and your wife can be with him when I talk to him. That's all I ask."

Bromley nodded, paused while Slattery turned the knob and pulled the door open.

The shots came in the moment the old man stepped past Slattery onto the porch. Two shots, so quick in succession they blasted as one. Slattery, in plain view in the doorway, felt a hot streak of pain slash above his left ear as his hat was ripped back off his head. The second bullet smashed the glass beside his shoulder.

It took a fraction of a second for Slattery to jump forward onto the porch.

"Down! Down!" he yelled at Bromley, standing stiffly erect and stunned in plain view. Another bullet banged out. Slattery shoved the old man down the steps and behind the cover of the wooden porch.

Chapter Seven

Slattery fell flat beside the wheezing, panting Bromley, hearing the steel slug smack solidly into a porch timber. Bromley began to push himself up onto his hands. "Still! Lie still!" Slattery warned. "He's still over there."

He brushed one hand above his ear, felt the warm stickiness of the blood that wet his hair. He wiped his fingers on his trousers, inched his head up and peered across toward the opposite buildings. With the moonlight blocked by the roofs, the alleyway between the general store and jeweler's was pitch black. He could make out nothing, no form of a man, no movement. Along Center shouting had started and the confused clomping of running feet.

"Tom! Catch the gun, Tom!" Charlie Raine was pressed against the wall left of the open doorway, the Starr revolver in his fingers, ready to throw it outside.

"Keep it low," Slattery said. He raised his head a little more, brought up one hand to catch the weapon.

A bullet banged out from the alleyway, zinged past Slattery's ear.

Ducking back, Slattery didn't take his eyes from the Starr, its silver barrel flashing in the porch lamplight while it sailed through the air. It struck the top step and bounced into the dust five feet from Slattery.

He lay prone, crawled forward, his right arm outstretched for the weapon. A bullet sang across the street's width, then another, both kicking up small mushrooms of dirt inches from the revolver.

Slattery gripped the barrel, yanked it in. Yells came from all directions now, excited calls and questions. The sound of running was closer, more confused, making it seem as if all Gunnison was boiling out, terrified; everyone was heading for the center of the town. A savage thrust of fear drove through him. He knew what one wild bullet could do, and there were women and children out in the street too.

"Keep the people back," he said to Bromley. "Keep them away from the alley." Crouching, he aimed the .45 and fired once into the alleyway.

He didn't wait for return fire, but moved forward, still hugging the stairs for cover. He put the second shot in low against the general store.

He zig-zagged, expected a bullet from the bushwhacker, his weapon aimed into the thick blackness to catch the barrel flash.

But no shot came.

His slug whacked into the building's clapboards, ricocheted with a loud whine deep into the depths of the alley. Slattery reached the boardwalk, went up and across and threw himself against the jeweler's front wall.

The thump of boots was loud back there. Slattery slid around the corner, bent low, then kept moving. No sound ahead, only the noise behind him in the street. Close to the rear he slowed, pressed himself against the jeweler's. Beyond the right corner a door slammed shut.

Slattery waited long seconds before he rounded the corner and broke from the deep shadows into the moonlight.

No lights shone from the line of closed doors in the rear of the buildings. The bank was a block away on the left, the Frontier Saloon on the right. Slattery ran to the right.

Ke knew the Frontier's small back storeroom, piled high with beer barrels and wooden crates, with a few card tables spotted about the floor. He jerked the door open, watchful of a shot which could come from behind anything in the room. Light streaked out beside his boots. The room's front door was open to the bar. He could see only one man in there—Horse Owens—sitting at a wall table, a bottle and glass in front of him.

Slattery touched his head, felt the blood had ceased its flow and was already caked along the ear. He moved past the beer barrels and card tables into the bar, the Starr thrust out, cocked.

The saloon was one long room with a high, half-frosted plate glass window on both sides of the batwings. Bottles and shot glasses still dotted the counter of the mahogany bar, left there by the drinkers who'd piled out into the street. Len McEneny, a thin man with thick black hair, a rather long nose and a careful lipless mouth, stood near the back bar mirror. He saw Slattery enter. His eyes flicked to Horse Owens, warning him.

Horse turned his big head, the glass in his hand poised near his mouth. His initial irritated stare gradually changed to a frown as he watched Slattery jam the Starr into his waistband. Unconsciously, Horse fingered the wide white bandage across his nose.

"What in hell you want," he asked sullenly.

"You didn't go out to watch the shooting, Horse?"

The huge cowhand set down the glass impatiently, slurping beer over the rim onto the table. "I figured someone'd go after you sooner or later. Don't cry 'bout it to me."

Slattery walked closer to the table. The clicks of bootheels and excited talk bounced in from the porch. Faces had appeared at the windows, noses and foreheads pressed close to the glass. "Lay your gun on the table," he said.

Horse Owens waved one big hand in the air. "Listen, Slattery—"

"Flat on the table," Slattery said. "Now."

Neither man spoke for a moment, both motionless in the brightly lighted room. Faces lined the tops of the batwings, and a few had crouched down in order to see from underneath. Gus Loheed, with his forearms folded into a wedge, pushed and shoved his way through the crowd, throwing men aside in his haste to get in. He banged open the swinging doors and came straight toward Slattery. Martin Bromley was a step behind the lawman.

Owens watched Slattery carefully. He'd let his right hand drop slowly to his side, and it came up as carefully with his six-gun. He laid it flat on the table.

He revolved the drum, so everyone could see the weapon was fully loaded. "You got the wrong man," he said. He spoke calmly, never taking his eyes from Slattery's face. "You're pushin' me, Slattery. Too much, you're pushin' me."

Gus Loheed halted at the table. His glance moved from the revolver to the coagulated blood on Slattery's head and ear. "You see who did it, Tom?"

"I know who did it."

"It wasn't me," Owens said. "I was in here. He looked at the bartender. "That right, Len?"

The bartender's long-nosed face nodded. "He was in here, talkin' with Matt Ellson. He was right in here."

"Slattery called me, Loheed," Owens cut in angrily. "I don't like a man callin' me. He'll know it when I go after him."

Loheed eyed the fully-loaded drum, listening to the temper of the onlookers. "Doc'll fix that up," he told Slattery.

Slattery looked at the lawman. "That all, Gus?"

"You didn't see who it was," Loheed answered. "Martin here says he couldn't see, either."

"He was on top of me," Bromley offered. "I couldn't tell. I couldn't see a thing."

Slattery exhaled, gave a slow nod. He turned and started for the doorway. Loheed stepped quickly to his side, then ahead of him to go through the batwings first. He had the tips of his fingers against the slats when the expressions on the watchers' faces changed abruptly.

"Slattery! Damn you, turn, Slattery!"

Slattery saw the heads pull back, heard the mad scramble of bodies suddenly thrown aside, shoving those behind toward him. He reached for the Starr's butt while he threw himself to the left, crashing into a table and taking it down with him.

Owens, standing straight and looking as tall as the ceiling beams, fired the gun in his hand once, twice.

The thick circular top of the table took the bullets meant for Slattery. Rolling away, he brought up the .45, steadied it and thumbed the hammer. A roaring concussion threw him still more off balance.

Slattery's bullet struck Owens square in the chest. He stopped short, amazed shock covering his broad face. The six-gun slipped from his grip, dropped to the floor.

Owens swayed where he stood, swore at Slattery. He tried to keep coming, but his legs gave and he plunged forward, hitting a chair and crashing down into it with a bone-crunching thud.

Slattery stood and moved back to the fallen man. He kneeled beside him.

"Horse," he said, "who put you on me?"

Owens' eyes rolled and focused themselves on Slattery. "You . . . You." His eyes closed.

Slattery gripped the man's shoulder. "Who, Horse? Who?"

Owens didn't make a sound. A convulsion shook his body and the shoulder slackened in Slattery's hand.

For a long moment Slattery stared at the dead man. Then, he rose to his feet. Beside him Loheed said, "I'll take that gun in my office, Slattery."

Slattery held out the weapon. "Take it now. I'll fix myself up. I don't need help."

"You'll come to my office. Both you and Martin Bromley'll come," said Loheed. He didn't accept the revolver, simply turned and walked from the room ahead of Slattery.

Once in his office Sheriff Loheed left Slattery and opened the iron-barred door that led to the cell block. The room was large with bare stone walls and gray-painted floorboards. Papers on the rolltop desk were arranged in a neat pile beneath a bone ashtray, and on the gunrack the line of rifles and shotguns were oiled and polished until they shone with a dull bluish sheen. Slattery didn't speak while he walked to the door and waited. Bromley, watching him, glanced worriedly out into Center.

"Maybe Gus will walk over to the restaurant with you," he offered. "I'll go with you, too."

Slattery followed the hotelman's stare. He'd been as much aware of the crowd while they'd come along the street, the angry-looking men, reluctant to give way to him. They waited the same way now, bunched together between the jail and saloon, faces tight and serious, craning their necks to see what went on inside the jail office. "I'll get back to my room alone, Martin. That isn't the help I need from you."

Loheed reappeared, holding Slattery's Win-

66

chester carbine in one hand and his filed-down Colt in the other. He came to the desk and, pushing the papers aside, laid the weapons flat.

"We'll get your roll and then you leave town," he said.

"You saw Owens throw down on me, Gus. And you're still running me out?"

"I'm not running you out. You're leaving on your own."

"I'm not leaving unless you run me out." He backed away from the desk, didn't pick up either of the weapons. "I'm going to do what I came back to do."

Their stares locked. The veins in Loheed's neck seemed to tighten as he walked to the front window and stared through, yet he said nothing. Slattery was puzzled. Loheed hadn't hesitated the night he'd taken him in five years ago, nor when he'd taken his guns away today. His expression didn't hold the hate of the crowd, but something different. Not anger, nor an absence of hostility either, but something more guarded.

In the silence that stretched out, Martin Bromley said, "If you talked to Freddy, would you leave after that? You wouldn't bother us?"

"I never meant to bother you. Just to talk to Fred about MacCandles."

Loheed came back to the center of the room and stood there as though he was trying to make up his mind. Martin Bromley had shifted his stare to the lawman.

"You didn't have proof MacCandles . . ." Loheed began.

67

"I've got all the proof I need." Slattery motioned with one hand toward the saloon. "You heard McEneny say Matt Ellson was with Horse before I was shot at. You know as well as I do MacCandles was behind it."

"Dammit, MacCandles hasn't been in town all this week," Loheed snapped. "He proved at the trial he wasn't near town that night."

"Oh, hell," Slattery said. "MacCandles doesn't make a move without covering. He knew I'd be looking for Freddy tonight. He was having a dance out to his place so he'd have plenty of witnesses to back his story about Freddy not being there."

"A dance?" Bromley had reached into his coat pocket for his handkerchief, but he stopped. He watched Slattery with a strained, listening look. "I didn't know anything about a dance." His words fell off.

Slattery turned from the hotelman to Loheed. "If you're running me out, I'll take my things. You decide."

"You've done nothing to be run out for." Loheed stood with his feet apart, thinking and still staring at Slattery. Finally, as if he'd decided what he'd been pondering, "I'll take that six-gun, too. On the desk."

Slattery drew the revolver and laid it beside the Colt. "You make bushwhackin' damned easy, Gus."

"It won't be if you stay in that room up there."

"Or if you handled the street the way you used to, Sheriff."

At that Loheed's face became rigid. The expression was similar to the one he'd shown when he'd come out of the cell block. Only it was more pronounced this time. Slattery breathed in deeply. Up to now, he'd held back from pushing. He'd wanted to do his proving within the law. Now, he decided he had a right to apply pressure. And he knew where he would start. He made no further remark, simply swung around and went outside and along the boardwalk.

The sheriff returned to the window and stood there looking out. He rubbed his mustache as his eyes followed Slattery closely. In the long silence Martin Bromley wiped his forehead with his handkerchief.

"Slattery won't cause trouble out there," he said in a serious voice. "You don't have to watch him like that."

Loheed merely nodded. "He can't depend on any of us. Not even me. He knows that now."

"It's the only way it can be, Gus. We all knew that."

Suddenly Loheed swore. He said with a bitter smile, "I know what I'd do, Martin, if I didn't have Kathleen and the kids."

Martin Bromley nodded thoughtfully. "He'll give up looking for Freddy in a few days," he said slowly. "He won't want to stay here after he does."

Loheed gave no answer. He sucked in a deep breath, concentrated his attention on the men outside who stood along the walks and porches, watching Slattery cross Center toward the restaurant.

Chapter Eight

Slattery had already reached the boardwalk which fronted the restaurant porch. In the brightness of the moonlight and the stars, he could easily see he was being watched, but he ignored that now. No danger would come from these people who showed their feelings so openly. Any future threat would come as it had from the alleyway, not right in the main street with the sheriff watching his every move. He'd taken a good look at those lined along the saloon's porch, had gotten a quick glance inside when one or two of the men had pushed through the batwings. Matt Ellson was the person he hunted, but he wasn't at the bar or at one of the front tables.

The men on the porch steps parted to let him through. Over their hats he saw that Ellen Hasslett and Charlie Raine waited in the doorway. Ellen stood on her tiptoes, watching him anxiously. She moved aside to let him enter the dining room, but her eyes didn't leave the side of his head.

"That must hurt," she said. "It's still bleeding a little."

"It's all right. Won't take long to fix." He looked at Raine. "Thanks for the gun, Charlie."

Raine nodded, and Ellen said, "I'll heat water, Tom. I'll put it up in the room."

"Cold water'll be enough," Slattery told her. "You don't have—"

"I want to," she said. "It'll be easier with warm water." She shuddered and tried to soften his hard eyes with a smile. "It'll only take a few minutes."

She went past the swinging doors. Slattery walked behind Charlie Raine to the counter. "Have you still got the bay you used to keep in the barn?" he asked.

Raine simply nodded. "I don't ride him much now, since the leg's stiffened up."

"Could you have him saddled for me in about an hour? And a gun?"

Charlie scratched his bony jaw slowly. "I haven't got a gun, Tom. Look, let it go. There's talk you were out to MacCandles' place tryin' to cause trouble. You won't get anywhere facin' him out there."

"When I face MacCandles, he'll be right here in town so everyone can see," Slattery said. He glanced at the wall clock. It was five minutes to ten. "I'll come around to your place in a half-hour."

Raine nodded, did not answer. When Slattery turned toward the kitchen, the thin old cook limped from one table to another, arranging the chairs neatly in place before he locked the front door and closed up for the night.

Slattery dabbed a corner of the wet towel against the side of his head. Owens' bullet had scraped away hair and skin, and the raw flesh burned as he cleaned the blood and dirt that had

71

caked over the wound.

"You should have Doctor Gingras bandage that," Ellen said. She'd waited in the doorway, not speaking until blood started to seep from the open cut. "I'll get him."

"No. It's all right." He looked around, and a sharp twitch of pain flashed along the tendons of his neck. "Since you've owned this place, has Freddy Bromley come in here often?"

"Yes. Most of the younger people did, on weekends especially. After the socials and dances."

"Did you ever hear him say anything about the Nye killing? Or the trial?"

"No," Ellen answered, frowning. "None of them said anything about that until a month ago. I was a stranger, and they don't get close to strangers."

"You've been here four years."

"I was still a stranger. There people are so afraid of talking out in front of anyone they don't know, it takes years before they trust you. But for the last six months, I've heard nothing but talk about you."

"How much of it was connected to Mac-Candles?"

"None that I heard. It was all about you and Nye and Freddy Bromley. Especially Freddy. As if everyone expected you'd ride right into the hotel and shoot him."

She stepped forward and unfolded a fresh towel and took the soiled one from Slattery. The motions put an end to the conversation. While Slattery pressed the clean cotton over his ear, he was silent. He drew the towel away, watched in the

72

mirror to see if blood still seeped. He had to stop any flow before he left, but not with a bandage. White cloth would show up in the dark.

"That affair MacCandles was having at his ranch," Ellen said. "Some of the people from the west end would have gone. I could go up to my house and see if anyone noticed Freddy out there."

"They wouldn't've seen him unless MacCandles wanted them to," Slattery told her. "He was putting on a big show of innocence about anything that might've happened to the kid. He had his own woman and all, a really beautiful one I'd never seen before. Whatever he was trying to sell to those people, he sold. You wouldn't learn anything from them."

Her eyebrows rose and she shook her head. "That MacCandles..." She sounded casual, but she was choosing her words with care. "Don't blame the people. He controls the bank and he can ruin their businesses any time he wants. His cattle have made this a real stop on the railroad, and his hired hands keep the saloons and stores going. Gus Loheed is sheriff only as long as he doesn't step on Circle M toes. There's hardly a man in this town who doesn't have to jump when MacCandles speaks."

"You haven't jumped."

Ellen's shoulders moved in a shrug. She took a long swallow before she answered. "I told you what he tried. This place was bought with the money my father left me."

"And when it's gone? MacCandles is good at

73

giving things time to happen."

She paused, and he waited, eyeing the wound in the mirror. No blood spotted the towel now. Outside on Center a buggy rolled noisily past and the creaking and rumble of the wheels slowly died with the hoof beats. Ellen shot one glance at him, looked away.

"What then?" he prompted.

"I won't stay," she said. She emphasized the answer with an irritated toss of her shoulder. "I don't have to bow any more than you do." She moved a step closer to him, her eyes wide and troubled. "I've wanted to see someone who'd stand up to MacCandles. I'd gotten so sick and tired of waiting."

"I haven't stood up to him, Ellen. He wouldn't even admit I was a direct threat to him out there."

Again her head shook. "Just coming back here you've faced him." She was so close to him he could smell her lavender perfume, could feel the warmth radiating from her. Her chin was raised, and her lifted face was shining. "When you leave, I'll go. I don't want to stay here any longer."

Slattery dropped the towel beside the basin, began to shake his head. "No, Ellen."

"You could leave right now," she said, laying her hand on his arm. Her fingers trembled and she gripped tighter. "You've shown this town you told the truth. You've got nothing to be ashamed of."

He stood without moving, looking down at the part in her hair, clean and neat like a child's. "I've proved nothing, Ellen. I still have to prove that."

"Against MacCandles' hired guns? The whole

town and country?" She jerked her head back. "I've watched how he gets rid of the men he doesn't want. Either Owens beats them out in that street, or Gillman or Matt Ellson goes after them with a gun. You haven't even got a gun. I don't want that for you."

Her arm dropped and circled his back. She pressed against him. The sudden drive of feeling melted the reserve he'd tried to keep between them. Now, in an instant, the years alone in a prison cell, away from the closeness and warmth of a woman, were gone. His arms went around her, drew her to him.

She was on her tiptoes, lips ready, her fingers tight, moving up along his back to his neck. Her whole body arched against his, responding to the kiss. He felt everything else driven from his mind, the streets and town outside, MacCandles. There was nothing but the burning, long, breathless moment.

Her fingers loosened, and she edged him back toward the center of the room, leading him but allowing him to lead. Slattery's eyes rested on the iron posts of the bed. He stopped, both hands gripped tight against the smooth softness of her back. What could happen would come from their loneliness, their worry, the pressure of the hate and violence that was around them. It was MacCandles and Gunnison, squeezing them until everything came too suddenly, not as it should. He wouldn't let MacCandles or the town do that.

"Ellen."

Her body slackened, and she buried her face

75

against his chest. "I know," she said, her voice muffled and shaky.

"Not this way," he said. "It isn't what we really want. Either of us."

She nodded, drew back slightly, rested against his arm. "But I'm not sorry. I meant what I said. When this is over."

"It'll be over." He let her go and she moved out of his embrace. Her small shoulders rose and fell with her breathing. Her pretty face was dry, terribly serious. "You won't run, Tom. You won't hide. What'll you do without a gun?"

"I'm not sure." And, when she opened her mouth to speak, he took her arm. "You've been hurt enough through me downstairs. You've still got to live."

Ellen nodded, didn't speak until he'd moved with her to the doorway. Her head shook back and forth, reluctant to leave without knowing what he would do.

"Tom. If you decide. If I can help, I'll be at my house. Next to the Bromley's. I'll wait."

Nodding, he released his fingers from her arm. "It helps just to know. Don't worry now."

He closed the door behind her, then stepped close to the window shade. Loheed would be watching to see he stayed inside. One of MacCandles' men would be right on the job, too. He'd have to wait a little while before leaving, so there'd be no chance of his being followed this time.

Chapter Nine

Clouds had blown down from the north in the last half hour before midnight. The moon, so bright through the early evening, was veiled and heavy as a herd of thick black thunderheads grazed across the sky. Far off on the horizon, jagged flashes of lightning cut through the blackness. Slattery had pulled up his bay mount in the cover of the willows, had sat for the past ten minutes watching the Circle M.

He could make out just slight outlines, for the sprawling buildings had a more concealed look than he'd seen earlier. Yellow lamplight illuminated only two windows in the bunkhouse and the kitchen of MacCandles' home. Not one of the lights was bright enough to throw its reflection across the sandy width of the yard. If MacCandles had a man on guard, he'd catch the sound of a horse or a boot easily before anyone got close enough to do damage.

Slattery spoke softly to the bay and turned into the wagon road. The prairie wind that whistled through the close brush broke the stillness. Somewhere beyond the Platte's lower bank, the warbling call of a night bird sounded. Slattery dismounted before he reached the yard so his horse would stay downwind from the ranch animals. As he ground-tied the bay, he saw a shadow pass the back window of the bunkhouse.

He approached the long wooden building from the rear, then slid along close to the window and peered inside. Young Billy Ellson sat at the table in the middle of the cluttered room. His head and shoulders were bent over the cards he'd set out in a game of solitaire.

Carefully, Slattery worked his way around to the front of the building. He halted again at the corner, listened, became sure no one watched the yard. He turned the knob. Billy Ellson glanced up. Instantly a terrified stare covered his freckled face.

"Just sit," Slattery said. "Keep playing." The doorlatch clicked behind him, and he moved to a holstered gun draped across the second bunk.

Billy Ellson fumbled with the cards. Slattery drew the Colt, checked its load, then jammed it under his belt buckle.

"That's my gun. You c'n have it," Billy said. He tried to control the shaking fingers but couldn't. "Go 'head, take it."

"Where's your brother?" Slattery asked.

"He ain't here. He rode out with Mr. Mac-Candles. They took the Forsythe woman back to her father's ranch."

"Who's in the house?"

"No one. I'm the only one they left here. Just me." Billy's eyes flicked fast to the door, his face showing more of a terror now. Slattery edged aside. He caught the sound of footsteps outside in the yard. "The cards," he whispered. "Play those cards." His fingers gripped the Colt's butt, and

Billy's head snapped down. He fingered the cards, set one on the second pile. The door opened and Matt Ellson walked inside. "Hole's dug," he said. "They'll be comin'—" His words broke off at the expression of his young brother's face. He whirled on his boot heel, let his right hand fall toward the six-gun.

"Hold it. Just like that," Slattery ordered, jamming the Colt's muzzle into Matt's stomach. He jerked the six-gun from its holster, threw it onto the bunk.

Matt stiffened, glanced from his brother to Slattery. "What in hell you tryin'?" he said hurriedly. "You were told to keep off this spread."

"Open the door and go outside slow. We're going back to town."

Matt stared at him with a questioning frown. "I don't go nowhere. Not with you, I don't." Moving quickly, he reached out to slap the Colt barrel away.

Slattery side-stepped, brought up his left and smashed a vicious backhand across Matt's jaw. Matt stumbled and banged against the wall.

Billy was on his feet, the chair shoved out from under him crashing to the pine floor. All the fear had vanished from his face, was replaced by a wild, bitter hate. "You don't touch him again!" he threatened. "You don't touch either of us!"

Slattery waved the muzzle. Billy slowed. "Cut it," said Slattery's soft voice. "Quit that yelling or your brother gets it first."

"Don't. Don't, kid," Matt warned. And when Billy halted, "Tell MacCandles what happened.

79

Don't try anythin' on your own. MacCandles'll handle it."

"But he's got nothin' on you, Matt. He ain't."

"Tell MacCandles Matt's going to explain what he was talking to Horse Owens about before I was bushwhacked."

Billy's shoulders seemed to sag. He gazed hopelessly at his brother. "Matt?"

"Forget it, kid. He's pullin' a bluff." He silenced as Slattery grabbed his shoulder. The drumming of horses' hoofs was loud outside from the flat behind the barn. Those in the lead were already in the yard when Slattery's arm pulled Matt behind the door with him. Slattery gestured to Billy. "Sit at the table. Make it look as if you're still playing cards."

Talk went on beyond the door. Boots thumped on sand as the riders dismounted. The kick of footsteps came to the bunkhouse and the door opened inward.

It was Nate Gillman. He didn't close the door, went directly to Billy. "Come on, kid. We're all set." His entire body became taut when he looked into Billy's face. He began to turn.

"Slow," Slattery said quietly from the cover of the door. "Tell the rest to come in. All of them."

Gillman's face was calm, cautious. Slattery said, "Quick. You'll get it first. Straight in the stomach."

"Mr. MacCandles," Gillman said. "Come in here for a minute. All of you, come in."

MacCandles' voice said, "What is it?"

"This kid here." He swung half around at Billy.

"You better come in." He stared out the doorway, his eyes narrowed but controlled.

Boots shuffled on the sand, low talk, then, "Okay, inside you," MacCandles said to someone.

Freddy Bromley entered the room first, with MacCandles a step behind him, followed by a rangy, olive-skinned cowhand Slattery hadn't seen before. Freddy was tall and slender with short-cropped yellow hair that made him seem younger than fourteen at the trial. Now, his face bruised and swollen along one cheek and his mouth, he had an older, more worried appearance than his nineteen years. His eyes opened wide in surprise when Slattery pushed the door shut. MacCandles glanced from the boy to the others, his hard handsome features giving away nothing. Gillman had edged to the left to make room. The dark-skinned man halted on the right and stood with one hand poised above his holstered gun, watching and waiting like a wary dog.

Freddy went to move closer to Slattery. Not sure of him, Slattery waved him away. "Slattery, they were going to kill me," the boy said. "They had me tied up over to Ellson's line cabin. They were going to do it here."

"That's ridiculous," MacCandles said. He smiled faintly, but it didn't change the frown on his face.

Gillman said, "We can get him, boss. He can't take us all at once."

"Don't move," MacCandles told him, his voice cold and clipped. He added as though simply talking business, "What do you want, Slattery?"

"He's taking Matt into Gunnison," Billy said.

81

"He's got some fool idea Matt put Horse Owens up to goin' after him."

"Horse Owens?" MacCandles repeated, considering the words.. "He was alone when he shot at you."

"Matt did send Horse after you," Freddy Bromley said. "I heard them talking about it. They've got Sid Lewis waitin' outside town now in case you tried comin' out tomorrow." He stepped quickly past Gillman. "I wrote to you, Slattery. I tried to help you. Please get me out of here."

MacCandles said, "Go ahead, Slattery, take him with you. You can use anything he tells you. All he has to say is he saw Horse Owens cut back of the hotel right after the Nye killing."

Slattery looked directly at Freddy. "That right?"

Freddy rubbed his bruised jaw, touched his swollen lips carefully. "They made me talk. They had me tied up and they made me."

"That's all, Slattery," MacCandles said. "You came out for Freddy. Now you have him. Both of you get away from here."

"I came after Ellson this time."

"You don't get him. Feel lucky I'm letting you ride out. Take Freddy-boy and his ridiculous story that we were going to kill him. Now, Slattery. Unless you want to take on the five of us."

Silence came then, stretching out while MacCandles took a step back toward the wood stove. It's a bluff, Slattery thought. A sudden outbreak of gunfire would be heard across the river, and MacCandles was too smart to allow a chance of anyone knowing about this. But Slattery knew he was only fooling himself. He could die right here; he could sense it in MacCandles' reflective manner and the cold watching sets of eyes.

"Get outside," Slattery told Freddy Bromley. "My horse's around back. Bring him up." Freddy opened his mouth to say something and Slattery's voice hardened. "Now. Get going."

Freddy turned the knob. He left the door wide open when he stepped into the yard.

"Dammit, Mr. MacCandles," said Matt Ellson. "We can take him."

"You wait," MacCandles said calmly. "All of you."

Horse's hoofs kicked the sand. Slattery backed to the threshold keeping the Colt centered at MacCandles' heart. "Come into the doorway, MacCandles," he said. "So I can see you."

MacCandles did not move.

The hammer of Slattery's weapon clicked. "You set up my father and my brother. I wanted to do this legally, but I don't care how it's done, MacCandles."

For an instant MacCandles stood perfectly still. He remembered seeing Slattery that night after the gunfight. He'd gotten into town too late to save the two cowhands he'd had waiting for Slattery, and he'd gone directly to the jail. Despite the beating the mob had given him, Slattery had had this same dangerous, threatening look.

Slattery called over his shoulder, "Drive their horses off, Freddy. Wait near the crick." He lifted the muzzle inches, directly into the rancher's face.

83

MacCandles stepped slowly to the doorway, stood there silhouetted in the glare of the lamplight while Slattery stepped back to the bay and mounted.

He kneed the horse toward the flat, sitting half-turned in the saddle, the Colt leveled until he and the animal blended with the night.

The moment the bay's hoofbeats died out, Matt Ellson, gun in hand, came through the doorway and headed for the rear of the bunkhouse.

"No, don't shoot, you stupid fool!" MacCandles snapped. "I don't want any shooting here."

"They'll get back to town."

"They won't reach town. You head around back and see which way they go."

Ellson turned the corner. MacCandles faced Billy and the olive-skinned cowhand. "Chino, you and the kid saddle the horses in the barn. Gillman, you go into the house and put more lights on."

"Sure, boss."

"Damn you, keep that 'boss' stuff to yourself. Move."

Gillman ran toward the house. MacCandles walked around to the side of the bunkhouse. Matt Ellson stood in the yellow square of lamplight that slanted down from the rear window. "Get out of the light," MacCandles said, "unless you want to be their first target."

"They're just ridin', Mr. MacCandles. They're crossin' the river to the other side." He was visibly uneasy, hands never still, rubbing his right palm hard against the handle of his six-gun.

"I gave you credit for more brains than letting everyone see you talking to Owens," MacCandles said coldly. He wiped one hand wearily across his mouth, his concern showing on his face, jowls tight. Thunder grumbled far to the north, and he stared at the southern sky, almost completely clouded over. Thin shafts of moonlight sliced through the scud miles below the Platte, but the flat siding both river banks was black dark. "You do nothing on your own from now on. None of you do. Do you hear?"

"Yes. I hear, Mr. MacCandles."

Chino was coming from the barn leading two horses. Most of the windows on both floors of the house were brightly lighted, making it look as if there was someone in every room. Gillman appeared on the porch. He held MacCandles' silver-plated Spencer carbine. When he reached the pinto Chino had saddled, he slid the weapon into the boot.

"I figured you'd want this, Mr. MacCandles," he said.

MacCandles gestured at the barn. "Hurry in there and see what's holding up that kid. Bring those horses out here."

Gillman ran for the high barn doorway. Mac-Candles walked straight to the pinto, checked the cinch, then swung up into the saddle. "Chino and I will head straight for town. They know Sid Lewis is spotted somewhere near there so they'll have to slow down. We'll work out from Foye's blacksmith shack and flush them back toward you. You be watching."

"We will," Matt Ellson said. He slapped his six-gun. A faint cold smile twisted his lips. "We don't hear you, we'll circle 'round the other side of town. They might try goin' in that way."

MacCandles nodded. "This time don't let anyone see either of you," he said. "This whole trouble never would've started if you'd been careful enough last time. You make damned sure you remember that."

Chapter Ten

"Why didn't you say something about it at the trial?" Slattery said. "That was the time to help me. With Owens dead, it doesn't help at all."

"I don't know. I didn't think it was connected, at first. But I thought about it all the time you were away. And I wrote you."

Slattery nodded in the darkness. He rode within two feet of the boy, close enough for Freddy's hazy figure to assume a definite shape in the saddle. He couldn't be sure of Freddy's expression, but he believed this was the truth. They'd stayed at the edge of the flat, using the river timber and brush to screen them from the opposite bank, letting their mounts make their own speed in the blackness. Slattery half-turned, strained to catch any sound, but there was nothing except an occasional boom of thunder. Lightning flashes were closer, illuminating the plain for seconds at a time. Still nothing. Yet he kept his hand near his belt, waited for any telltale noise or yell which could come. Freddy stared ahead like a jockey, body bent over, tense, wrists cocked tight on the reins.

"You've been hanging around with young Ellson," Slattery said shortly. "And out to Mac-Candles'. Did you tell them out there about the letter?"

"No. I didn't tell anyone. Not even my folks. They heard when the word started going around town I'd sent it. I don't know who found out. But MacCandles knew right to the day I mailed the letter."

"You told him exactly what you told me."

"The same thing. He had Chino and Lewis take me to the branding camp and hold me. That's where I got this face."

Slattery didn't answer. The bay had become impatient at the approaching storm. He tugged at his bit. Slattery held him down, patted his neck. "Easy, boy. Easy," he told him softly.

The horse kept tugging, and Slattery reached out and touched Freddy's shoulder. "Into the brush," he said. "Stop in there."

Freddy gave him a quick glance, a flick of the head toward Slattery while he swung his mount.

They pulled up behind two tall cottonwoods. Slattery strained his ears to listen. There was nothing but the crack of lightning. Whitish-blue light flashed over the water, through the brush, then died into black.

"See anything?" Slattery mumbled.

"No. Nothing."

"Thought I heard something."

They remained motionless, horses and riders, listening, watching. Gunnison was still a good two miles distant. They'd come across to this bank, knowing MacCandles' man Lewis waited close to the town. But how close, they couldn't know. Running off the Circle M horses had given them two, possibly three minutes.

"Horses," Freddy Bromley said. "Way out."

The clopping of running hoofs was barely audible beyond the opposite timber and brush. They didn't seem to be searching, but trying to reach the town first. "We'll cut off in another mile," Slattery said. "Circle around and edge in from the other side."

"Okay." Fear tightened Freddy's words, made him crouch even lower in the saddle as Slattery pushed his horse ahead of the boy.

Slattery watched him with sympathy. They had no way to tell how many men MacCandles could get to hunt them, or where they would be. Once Freddy got in with the story of his being held and beaten, MacCandles would be out in the open. The rancher would ring the town with guns to stop him. He could own enough men to do just that, Slattery thought. Even if they reached the hotel safely, Loheed couldn't be depended on. They had gone less than a mile when Slattery drew the bay in alongside Freddy Bromley's horse.

"You cut off here," he said quietly. "Kearney Crossing has a U.S. Marshall. Get to him and bring him to Gunnison."

He could hear Freddy exhale a long breath. "Good," the boy began. "We can—"

"I'll keep going," Slattery said. "They'll be listening for us. I can keep them hunting long enough for you to get clear."

Freddy was silent.

"Let me get out of earshot," Slattery said. "They'll hear only my mount's hoofs."

He kneed the bay, started to move past a thick

black growth of willows and alders.

The shot came as a complete surprise. The sharp crash of a rifle banged instantaneously with a sound like a hand slapping hard on the neck of the bay. The animal gave a quick jerk of its head, whinnied in pain and began to go down.

Slattery made a desperate effort to swing out of the saddle, but the horse fell straight forward, taking him with it. Someone across the river shouted an order, his voice loud. Two rifles crashed as Slattery's right leg hit solid earth. The foot held and he threw himself to the right. Brush tore his hat off, the gravel scraped his face. He rolled fast to the right, hearing the bullets zip by overhead with the sound of cloth being ripped. One ricocheted hollowly from a tree, making a hateful, quavering noise.

"My arm! My arm, Slattery!" Freddy Bromley cried. He was a shadow in the black two yards away, crouched over in the saddle holding his horse steady. "They got my arm!" He began to slip toward the ground.

"Hold on. Hold on." Slattery pushed himself up. He hadn't felt any pain, but now on his knees, it sliced up the leg from his right ankle. He shoved violently, jumped to his feet, putting his weight on his left foot, limped after Freddy. "Hold on. I'll get you."

Another yell came from across the river the voice echoing through the brush onto the flat. Water splashed under the horse's hoofs that crossed toward them. Behind Slattery the boy's iron shoes pounded the earth while the wounded animal kicked to right itself.

Slattery reached Freddy, gripped his shoulders and yanked him from the saddle. "Down, stay down," he said.

Straightening, he swung out wildly, slapped Freddy's horse's flank and started the animal running for the flat.

The bay was up, terrified, charging out of the willows after Freddy's mount.

"Run! Run!" Freddy cried. He'd gotten to his feet, was close behind Slattery.

"No, stay down. They'll follow the horses."

Three bullets pounded amidst the wild, confused splashing in the river. Steel slugs sang over Slattery's head and clipped the cottonwood leaves with a sharp snapping noise. One struck Freddy Bromley with a low, hardly audible thunk. He fell straight forward.

Slattery dropped to his knees beside the boy and reached out. He could hear the loud kicking splash of hoofs climbing the close bank. His hand touched Freddy's left arm. Blood wet the sleeve. His fingers crossed the shoulder, ran along the chest and were drenched with blood.

A horse rose up ten feet from Slattery, its rider straight in the saddle, rifle in his hands.

"The flat! They went for the flat!" Gillman shouted. Behind him a second horse appeared, then a third.

"Circle out left!" Matt Ellson yelled. "I'll go right!"

Another voice answered, muffled, unrecognizable. The three animals trampled past, smashed the brush, went through.

Slattery's fingers had found the wound, high up on the left side of Freddy's chest. He had the vein that pumped the blood and was pressing between there and the heart.

Freddy moaned, tried to roll over. "No. Lie still," Slattery whispered. "Still, Freddy." Painfully, he bent low over the boy, keeping his weight on his own left side. He had to stop the flow of blood, then move Freddy from here. Once Ellson and the rest were close enough to even glimpse the two horses, it would be easy to figure where they dropped off.

Slattery pressed the vein with one hand, jerked his shirt from below his pants with the other. He began to tear at the tail for cloth to use as a tourniquet and bandage.

"Neither of them!" Billy Ellson called. "Both saddles are empty!"

Matt Ellson cursed. "They must've driven them out of the brush. Gillman, you were first up the bank."

Gillman had jerked his claybank to a full stop, and now he swung back for the Platte. "Damn you, don't you yell at me. You keep your mouth shut to me."

"You were leadin'. Mr. MacCandles won't . . ." Matt killed his words, peered through the blackness.

Somewhere to the left running hoofs approached. Matt pumped his carbine, aimed it.

"They couldn't have another horse," Gillman.

"Shut up. We can't let anyone see us here like

92

this."

In less than a minute he could make out a horse and rider, and a second not far behind. From the tallness of the man and the way he sat his saddle, Matt knew it was MacCandles even before lightning flashed beyond the river, throwing enough of a glare for him to see clearly. And Chino was with him.

"Here. Over here, Mr. MacCandles," Matt called. "Over here."

The tall, hazy form drew up. Matt and Gillman turned their mounts toward the rancher.

"You get either of them?" MacCandles asked.

"Don't know," Matt told him. "Could'a got both of them. They might've fallen off."

"You fired enough bullets. We heard them close to town," MacCandles snapped. He swore, looked around in the direction of the river. "You didn't even see them."

"We got one. I know we got one," Gillman said. "I heard him yell."

Thunder boomed, loud in its nearness. The storm would strike full force in fifteen or twenty minutes, MacCandles knew. The lightning would give them visibility. He glanced across Matt Ellson's shoulder. Billy was riding up to them fast. He pulled his horse in beside his brother.

"There was blood on Freddy's saddle," he announced. "Not much, but there was blood."

"I knew we got one," Matt began.

"Quiet," MacCandles ordered. And to Billy, "Ride into town for Loheed. Tell him Slattery took the Bromley kid and we're hunting them. After, get around to the houses. Spread the word

93

Slattery shot him."

Billy hesitated, looked at his brother. "It's after midnight, Mr. MacCandles."

"I don't care what time it is. Get going. Do as I say."

"Get goin'. Get goin'," Matt said. "Do what the boss says."

"Sure. I will. Sure." Billy spurred his horse.

MacCandles watched the lightning flash, its brightness giving clear view of the humped irregular growth of the trees and brush that screened the river. Slattery would have moved the boy, if he was wounded, toward the town. A good mile distance separated him from Gunnison, with a wounded boy and no horse.

He'd made a mistake in not killing Freddy Bromley earlier, but he hadn't been sure he'd had all the information the kid had put in that damned letter. But things had gone wrong before. Everything could have fallen through the night Owens killed Nye. Nothing had been lost then. He'd taken his own action, had seen to it his other men were spotted exactly right so Slattery's father and brother would be cut down. The two men he'd put on Slattery had failed, but not the mob he'd had Matt Ellson build up.

Now, with Billy spreading the word, they could kill both the kid and Slattery the minute they had them.

"We'll flush them," he said. "Start on this side and work toward town. Five hundred to the man who finds them. A thousand to the one who kills Slattery."

Chapter Eleven

Slattery was in the middle of the river when he heard the horses coming back. Freddy had passed out while he'd worked to stop the flow of blood. He picked up the unconscious boy, realizing they'd be hunted now. Not positive of how many were after them, he knew their best weapon was concealment. He stepped slowly, carefully, through the sluggish channel and over the slippery rocks, his sore right leg straining under the boy's weight. The lightning flashes were nearer, brighter, the thunder almost overhead. He'd gained some time by crossing like this, but once the storm hit there was a good chance of being seen. High on the bank above him, cottonwoods, alders and willows loomed up black and still. He remembered a sheltered draw less than a mile west, a small stretch which ran back from the river into a hollow masked by trees. If he could make that, they'd have a chance. It would give cover from Mac-Candles and his gunmen, and from the storm.

He hadn't reached the higher rim of the bank before he realized the idea was hopeless. The running hoof beats were almost to the brush on the left bank. Slattery gripped Freddy tighter and crouched as he pushed through a thick growth of willows.

The voice that gave the orders belonged to MacCandles, he could tell; yet he couldn't clearly make out the words. Animals and riders moved quietly, holding down their own sounds to catch any noise he might make. A horse's hoofs splashed water, then a second set of hoofs. Two of them were coming across to this bank, possibly more.

He couldn't try to run, not with his heavy burden in his arms. And he'd make noises they'd hear.

Slattery hurried as fast as he could, deeper into the brush, using the hoof splashes to cover his movements. When he heard the horses kicking and wheezing to climb the bank, he backed into a thick stand of willows. Crouching low, he tenderly laid Freddy on the ground.

His hand felt across the makeshift bandage, touched the sticky warm blood. Too much blood had been lost already. The boy's shirt and jeans were soaked. Slattery pressed at the soggy bandage with his left hand. He drew the Colt, held it in his right.

The next bolt of lightning showed the closeness of the riders. Matt Ellson and Chino, Ellson in the lead, were in clear view. Both had six-guns ready while they stopped at each tree, each thick growth of bushes.

"Chino, swing out along the flat," Ellson called. "I'll work toward there."

"I'll flush him back toward you. You be ready."

"I'll be ready. Yell if you spot them. Just give a yell."

The hazy black form of horse and rider moved

96

off. Ellson came on, searching. Slattery crouched lower and shielded the unconscious boy with his body. The Colt was raised, aimed at Ellson's head. One trace of lightning and Ellson couldn't miss him. But he'd be a dead man before he could call out.

The horses's legs and flanks brushed the willows. The rider paused, slapped branches aside with his gun hand. Slattery's finger tightened on the trigger, held, then slackened as the animal and man moved on.

Slattery exhaled, drew in a long slow breath. Ellson had stopped again five yards away, was testing a clump of brush.

Lightning flashed.

Diagonally to Ellson's right, a twenty foot distance, a cluster of huge black rocks were bunched together near the edge of the river bank. Slattery made his plan as he lifted his hand from Freddy's chest. He wiped blood off on his coat, crawled like an animal toward the boulders.

Ellson was ahead of him. His back was to Slattery while he approached the rocks. Ellson stopped at the closest boulder, rode around it, searching, then continued on.

He became aware of Slattery a fraction of a second too late. The toe of Slattery's boot scraped on stone when Slattery jumped onto the large rock.

Ellson turned in the saddle, brought his six-gun around, but Slattery was on him.

Slattery smashed out with the Colt's barrel. The blow hit Ellson along the side of the head. He dropped his gun, folded forward and began to fall.

Slattery caught the man's shoulders, eased him to the ground and laid him between two huge boulders. Quickly, noiselessly, he took the bridle and led the horse back through the trees.

It took him almost a minute to get Freddy raised into the saddle, then to climb up behind him. He kneed the horse directly toward the flat, listening for any sound from Chino, watching for a lightning flash that could give him away.

The sound of the horse's hoofs falling and lifting in the sand seemed loud. Freddy's limp body slouched forward, threatened to slip. Slattery jammed the Colt under his belt and circled the boy with both arms. In the dead quiet he felt a cold wet drop touch his face, then another and another. Even the intermittent patter of the beginning rain seemed to him to be dangerous and loud.

"He's not on this side, Mr. MacCandles," Nate Gillman said. "I've gone a quarter mile. Even if they were running they couldn't've gone farther than that."

"We'll go across," MacCandles told him. "You go with Ellson."

MacCandles turned his horse down the bank. The raindrops had thickened and the full fury of the storm would hit within minutes. MacCandles took little notice of that. The lightning would help him and his men see, but he didn't depend on it. The weather was something to use, to be reckoned on, nothing more. He hadn't depended on the whims of the moon or sky or weather when he'd set up the Nye killing five years ago. He'd gotten control of every inch of country land north of the Platte by making the right decision at the right time. He'd put Slattery in jail long enough to allow himself to completely control Gunnison and its citizens. He'd find Slattery now, catch him and corner him and finish the job once and for all.

Somewhere on his left he heard voices talking. Jim MacCandles listened. He spurred his pinto out of the stream and up the sandy incline.

"Mr. MacCandles. Over here, Mr. MacCandles," Chino called.

Cold rain hit MacCandles' face as his horse broke through the willows. Lightning cracked and before the thunder boomed, he saw Matt Ellson and Chino standing near some huge rocks.

"He got Matt's horse," Chino said. "Jumped him."

"He hid behind the rocks, Mr. MacCandles. He come up from behind."

"All right. Climb up with Chino."

"But I—"

"Quick. Climb up." The rain hit then, with a tremendous crash of thunder, coming down in one solid sheet as though someone had overturned a gigantic bucket onto the trees and the flat. Ellson looked pathetic standing there, staring up at the rancher, drops of rain glistening in his hair and running down from his forehead in little rivulets to hang quivering from his nose. "You two'll go straight into town," MacCandles went on. "Show the people what you got trying to help Freddy."

MacCandles swung his mount, gestured at Gillman. "They'll head straight in. We'll circle around to the north and see Slattery doesn't try to hole up."

Once he was onto the flat he spurred his pinto into a gallop. A single trace of lightning was all he needed to tell Ellson's horse was not in sight. MacCandles rode on, waited until the long stretch of grass was illuminated again. His face was wooden, eyes narrowed in concentration. The instant he could see, he nodded, then he shouted over his shoulder.

"Straight in, Chino," he said. "As soon as we pass Byron Foye's place, you get Lewis and follow me into the sheriff's."

Chapter Twelve

Slattery had noted that lights were on in many of
the houses and buildings of Gunnison while he was
still five hundred yards from the town limits, too
many lights for four o'clock in the morning. Now,
as the storm struck with savage sodden violence,
the lights and shapes of buildings vanished as if a
dark curtain had been drawn over them. Slattery
held onto Freddy Bromley tighter, feeling the rain
drench the boy through to the skin. The cold
wetness didn't wake him. He stayed as limp and
helpless as he'd been all during the ride, and
Slattery had to grip the horn with both hands to
keep him from slipping.

A close flash of lightning threw twinkling, vivid
flame across the wind-blown grass, made the
buildings clearly visible for quick seconds. Blackness returned and the thunder boomed while
Slattery angled the horse toward the rear of the
hotel. The black darkness of the building made it
look larger than it was. Beyond its roof, the height
of the church steeple blended with the two-story
bank into a wall of darkness.

He didn't see anyone until he'd reined in near
the hotel's rear door. Slattery slid off the right side
and started to ease Freddy out of the saddle. He
had the boy in his arms, was adjusting his weight

when the blurry shapes of two men appeared from the alley. Both wore slickers. They halted and watched him.

"Get the doctor," Slattery called to them. "Tell him to come to the hotel. Freddy's shot bad."

The forms backed away and Slattery stepped through the mud toward the building. Before he'd reached the door it was thrown open and Martin Bromley looked out.

"Good Lord! How bad is he?" the hotelman asked hoarsely.

"We were trying to get back here," Slattery began.

"You shot our boy," Bromley's wife cried. She stood directly behind her husband, seemed aged and tired in her black dress. One look at her son and her voice rose shrilly, horrified. "Billy said you'd shoot him! You've killed him! You've killed him!"

"Helen," her husband said. "Open the bedroom." He stepped close to Slattery and took his son's left side. "Slow. Here, I'll back in first."

Slattery saw Billy Ellson now, standing just within the lobby doorway. He was talking to five men who were grouped around him, waving both arms in the air as though someone argued with him. "See there," he rasped. "Look at him. He shoots Freddy and he brings him in like that!"

Slattery said quietly, "I didn't shoot Fred, Mr. Bromley. MacCandles was going to have him shot and I got him away from the Circle M."

Bromley was silent, his face pale. They moved past the registration desk to the kitchen doorway, through that room, into a small bedroom.

Mrs. Bromley had the blanket pulled low. She stood motionless, hands clasped, white around the knuckles. "How is he? Is he dead, Martin?"

"He's breathing, Mother. Get some water and bandages."

She looked at Slattery. "This man," she said coldly. "This man shouldn't be in here."

"Get the water and bandages," her husband told her. "Watch for Doc Gingras."

The woman's shoulders sagged. She gazed from her husband to her son on the bed. She turned away, left the room.

Bromley bent over the boy. Freddy's breathing was slow, barely discernable, his skin drawn and waxy. His father leaned lower and unbuttoned the top of the blood-drenched shirt. "Billy Ellson ran in saying you'd made Freddy go with you. He said you'd shot him."

Slattery drew the Colt. "You knew I didn't have a gun. This had six bullets in it when I left Circle M. Smell it, Mr. Bromley. You'll see it hasn't been fired."

Bromley took the weapon, studied the cylinder, then raised it to his nose. He rubbed his jaw, thought about what Slattery had told him. The sound of footsteps in the kitchen made him glance around, and he saw Doctor Gingras hurry into the room.

The doctor was in his late sixties, bald, with a paunchy stomach. He was breathing hard from his run. He paid no attention to Slattery, set the black leather bag he carried on the bedside table and began his examination.

"Hot water," he said over his shoulder. "And some dry sheets, more blankets, too, Martin."

"The water's boiling now," Mrs. Bromley said. She'd followed the doctor in, and she laid the torn sheets she'd gathered for bandages on the edge of the bed. "I'll get the blankets."

"How bad is he, Doc?" Bromley asked.

Doctor Gingras' bald head didn't raise. "He's lost a great deal of blood. It's a wonder he's still breathing. Keep everyone out of here except your wife."

Slattery moved in front of the hotelman into the kitchen. Bromley made no motion to return the Colt. He stood as though he wasn't aware he still had it.

"Freddy went with you because he wanted to?" he said.

"Yes." Slattery told him rapidly what had happened at the MacCandles ranch. He spoke softly, aware of the loud confused talk that went on in the lobby. Bromley walked to the lobby doorway and stared out, but listened carefully. It was when Slattery mentioned what Freddy had stated about Horse Owens' being in the alleyway the night of the Nye killing that Bromley turned from watching the lobby.

Bromley said, "That's all he told you? That he saw Horse Owens?"

Slattery nodded. "It doesn't help. With Owens dead, it doesn't mean a thing."

Bromley stared directly into Slattery's eyes. "Would it have helped then? At the trial?"

"It could have. People would have remembered if they saw Horse. And who was with him."

Nodding, Bromley watched the doorway. Sheriff Loheed had appeared. Jim MacCandles was with him, and a crowd of town men bunched around close behind them.

Loheed halted on the threshold. "I'm taking you in," he said to Slattery.

"You'll hang for shootin' that kid," Billy Ellson shouted above the low talk. "We oughta lynch him right now," another voice cried. "Damn him, he oughta be strung up!"

Slattery lifted both hands away from his sides. "I'm not carrying, Gus," he said. "I didn't shoot Freddy."

MacCandles pushed Loheed aside. "He's a rotten liar," he snapped. "He took the boy from my place with that gun."

"That gun hasn't been fired," Slattery said to Loheed. "Mr. Bromley's seen that. You smell the barrel."

"That's right," Bromley said, his voice suddenly loud. He held the weapon up to Loheed's nose. "I don't know who shot my boy, but it wasn't done with this gun."

"Slattery shot him," MacCandles said savagely. "If the kid's dead—"

Slattery cut in. "He isn't dead. Doc'll bring him around, Sheriff. I'll stand on what Freddy has to say."

"I will too," Bromley said, looking into Mac-Candles' angry face. "I'll press no charges until I learn the truth." His glance rose, swept across the bunched faces. "Go on now, all of you. Let the doctor work."

"Carson and Fiske said Freddy was hit bad," a man said. "How is he, Martin?"

"Very bad. Let the doctor work. Please."

Loheed looked at MacCandles.

"All right," MacCandles said. "I'll wait. I'm staying in town to see Slattery faces up to this. I'll be over in McEneny's. My crew'll wait outside, Loheed, in case Slattery tries anything."

The rancher pushed his way through the crowd, trailed by the Ellsons, Gillman and Chino. The watchers began to move, conversing among themselves quietly. Outside thunder boomed, shook the room. Wind-whipped rain hissed against the kitchen window. Slattery waited until the doorway was clear, then he headed toward the lobby.

"Where are you going?" Martin Bromley asked.

Slattery did not answer, and the small elderly man grabbed his arm. He offered the Colt. "You'll need this. They'll be after you no matter what Freddy says."

"I hope they are," Slattery said. He whirled the revolver's drum, jammed the weapon under his belt and buttoned his coat. "I'll be back, Mr. Bromley."

Bromley followed him to the doorway, watched him go through the empty lobby. Before Slattery opened the front door the hotelman heard the rustle of his wife's starched dress behind him. He looked around at her and saw her mouth was set in a furious thin line.

"You took his side, Martin. What do you mean by taking that man's side?"

Bromley dodged her eyes, gazed in at the doctor bent over the bed. "He brought Freddy home. He wouldn't have done that if he was the one who shot him."

Her stare was unyielding. "What do you think people are going to say when they hear you helped the man who was after Freddy?"

"I don't care," the hotelman answered, dragging out the words. "I just want to know the truth. I want the truth now."

Mrs. Bromley shook her head, made no effort to comprehend his reasoning. "I don't understand you," she said. "Our son is close to dying in there."

"Helen, can't you see why?"

"I can see only that my son might die. It isn't a decent thing to give that man any help. It isn't decent."

Martin Bromley spoke slowly. "If we'd done the decent thing in the first place, Helen, our son wouldn't be in there like that." Now, for the first time he met her stare. "You're the only one who should know that better than I do."

"Tom. Wait, Tom."

The hail reached Slattery at the edge of the porch and, as he turned, he flicked open the button of his coat. Hurrying toward him along the boardwalk, her slim figure covered by a coat and shawl, was Ellen Hasslett. Slattery waited, watched the lighted window in the Frontier. The storm had slackened some but still was so thick the lamplight in the saloon and houses was blurred and hazy.

Rain beat against the porch roof, its steady noise loud in the quiet of the street.

"I heard MacCandles was after you," Ellen said. Her eyes were frantic while they rested on the traces of blood that spotted his wet coat. "You can see you're being watched."

"It's all right," he told her. "They won't bother me."

She stood with hands clenched, her clear eyes staring into his face. She looked even fresher and lovelier than in the restaurant, her soft long black hair glistening with raindrops against the background of the street lights. Her cheeks were flushed from her run. "I'll go with you and light a fire for you to dry off."

"I'm not going inside," he said slowly. "I'm going to talk to some people."

Ellen nodded quickly, as though she understood but she wished he'd listen to her.

"I know what you're planning," she said. "Don't force things any further. Please."

"I'm not sure what I'm planning myself, Ellen." Slattery's smile was oddly softened. It would be nice to go back with her, to get warm and dry, to talk. "If you're asked what we spoke about, say I was trying to find out who was with Horse Owens the night Nye was killed."

"Tom, that's the talk MacCandles wants you to spread. He's just waiting for a chance to get everyone after you. Those men are watching for their chance."

His face tightened. "You heard that?"

"Slim Lewis and Billy Ellson knocked on everyone's door. They said you'd shot Freddy and you were coming back to force a gunfight with Mac-Candles."

Slattery nodded. "Then you keep clear of me, Ellen. I want to be alone when MacCandles decides to move."

"But he won't be alone," she warned. Her eyes brimmed with tears. "He's got four or five men with him. And the town men. They all have their guns. I saw them."

"I'll be all right," he said. He stepped close to her, took her arm and began to walk her to the side of the porch. "Go ahead now," he said.

".You won't take any chances?"

"Ellen, I've got to face MacCandles sooner or later," he said quietly, intending to add more. But he stopped, fully aware of how she affected him now that he was close to her. His pulse sharpened, and a good warmth coursed through him. He kept his expression from showing that. "I appreciate this. Really. But I don't want you mixed up in anything."

She glanced across the street. "I don't care what they think. I've decided to leave no matter what happens. I will."

"I understand, Ellen." He caught the splash of footsteps in the darkness of the boardwalk, looked and saw Charlie Raine limp toward them from the adjacent block. The skinny old cook's head was bent out of the storm, his black coat flipping behind him in the wind. "Go ahead," he added. "I don't want either you or Charlie to end up in this." He left her and walked down the front steps.

Cold cutting rain slashed at his face, but the wetness made little difference in his sodden clothing. The lightning flashes were well south of the Platte now, the roll of thunder muffled by distance. He stepped carefully through the mud, not allowing the suck and pull to hold the boot on his weakened right foot and throw him off balance.

In the saloon window Matt Ellson's face was shadowed under the wide-brimmed hat he wore, yet he was unmistakable. His brother Billy and Chino were bare outlines beside him. Slattery sensed the tension which followed his movements, could feel its presence as one could feel the straining of a wire drawn too tight.

He walked on, watched, waited for anything. He did not know what would come, but he did know the open presence of MacCandles and his men in the town could start the first crack in MacCandles' armor. That hope, and the belief that his staying out here asking questions would force something, controlled his mind.

Charlie Raine did not speak to Ellen Hasslett. He had stepped off the walk when he saw Slattery hurry down off the porch. He didn't want to call out to Slattery and make the man stop in the middle of the street. He'd be more of an open target then; that's all Tom Slattery was, as far as Charlie could see, a wide open, shooting-duck target.

Some of the men had filed out through the batwings after Slattery passed. They stood together just out of the rain, watched Slattery go up onto the general store porch. Charlie began to move by them.

"Where you goin', Gimp?" Nate Gillman called. "You figure that bushwhacker needs help?"

"Yeah," Bob Patton said. He was a gangling man of thirty who clerked at the hardware store. "Raine thinks if he keeps Slattery alive, that boss of his'll take up with him. And he can get his business back without payin' too much."

The remark was picked up by the others, and it bloomed into low, angry laughter.

"It's almost two o'clock," Raine said loudly. "You all should be home with your families where you belong."

"We're where we belong," Patton said. "We know what we've got to do."

The grumbling died, was replaced by an instant intenseness. No one added a word. Most of the men didn't take their eyes from Slattery who was knocking on the front door of the general store. Lamps were on in the building's second floor where the Creightons lived. Those looking at the jail watched Gus Loheed in the doorway. The lawman followed what Slattery was doing as closely as everyone else.

Charlie wiped rain from his forehead. He continued on, limped toward the jail. Gillman's voice was sharp, high above the water striking the mud puddles. "Don't get into this, Gimpy. You stay out of it. Hear?"

"That's right, Raine. Don't push your luck."

Charlie Raine stepped up onto the jail walk, his limp less pronounced once he was out of the stickiness of the roadway. He halted at the door, still in the rain, his back kept to the Frontier porch.

"Those men are waitin' for a chance to jump Tom Slattery," he said. "You goin' to stop them, Gus?"

Loheed's eyes didn't shift from the general store. "They won't go after him out here."

"That's why they're waitin'. Jim MacCandles is makin' damned sure he isn't around so he c'n be blamed."

Loheed nodded his head. "That's right, Charlie. I can't do one thing to MacCandles unless I can prove he's after Slattery."

"So?"

"So, I'm standing here and letting the rest of them see me." The middle window in the general store second story was going up, and Slattery moved off the porch onto the walk to talk to Creighton. "They know I'm here. And so does Slattery."

"You're goin' to let it go at that?" Raine said sarcastically. "Just like when they gave Tom that beating?"

Loheed turned to him, his face became hard. "I brought Byron Foye and Horse Owens in for that. I kept that mob from takin' Slattery from the jail and lynching him.

Charlie Raine held down his desire to throw the facts into the sheriff's face. He remembered the

Gus Loheed of five years ago. His gun had tamed the first wild, lawless breed that had settled the county. Gunnison had grown so fast because of him. But that was before Jim MacCandles bought control of the river's north bank. The sheriff's office wasn't on the election ballot then, nor did Loheed have a family to consider. Raine understood all this. It was fresh in his mind when he answered.

"You had a few men who were willin' to back you then. This time—"

"There won't be another time if the trouble holds off 'till Freddy can talk." He stiffened where he stood, stared at the hotel. The doctor had come onto the porch, and the men were crowding off the Frontier steps to meet him.

Gillman and two or three in the lead spoke questions to the doctor, but he gave them no answer. He continued on past them, left them staring after him and talking together while he headed straight for the jail.

Loheed stepped down to the walk and met the doctor.

"The boy's dead, Gus," Doctor Gingras said. "I didn't tell that gang, but they'll find out." He shook his head. "You'd better get Slattery in right now."

"Did Freddy say anything?" Loheed asked.

"No, he never came around. He'd lost too much blood."

Loheed nodded, glanced through the thinning rain from the milling group of men in the street to

Slattery talking up to the storekeeper in the window. Loheed's face was wrinkled, concerned, as though he'd been dreading with fear and hopelessness that things would reach this point.

"Get off the street, Doc," he said. "You, too, Charlie." Then, he stepped down to the muddy roadway and walked toward where Slattery was standing.

Chapter Thirteen

Tom Slattery said to the storekeeper, "You were open late that night. I hoped you might be able to remember something. Just if you remember seeing anyone with Horse Owens."

Creighton's round mustached face was plain in the room's lamplight. "No, I didn't see Owens at all. I didn't see anyone." His gaze flicked up the street, returned to Slattery. "Go away and leave us alone."

Slattery was fully aware that Gus Loheed walked his way. He nodded to the storekeeper. "Mr. Creighton, I only want you to try to remember."

"No! I don't know anything. Go away. Leave us alone!" The head pulled back into the room, and the window came down with a heavy bang. The click of the window lock was loud, a quick, snapping noise above the splatter of the rain.

Slattery turned to meet the sheriff. Two of the men grouped in the street were going up the hotel steps. The rest made no attempt to hide the fact they kept a watch on Slattery. Slattery looked directly at the first home beyond the line of stores. His right hand brushed across his coat, fingered the middle button, the gesture of adjusting a weapon which might be underneath, automatic and businesslike. He wasn't certain that the Circle M cowhands had caught the movement. He wasn't certain that they realized exactly what he meant to do. He could only set the bait for one of them to come after him by knocking on every lighted door, and play it through from there.

"Get off the street," Loheed said before he reached Slattery. "Over to the restaurant."

"Gus, let me do this my way."

"Freddy's dead. You stay out here, that gang'll come after you."

An icy coldness ran through Slattery. He held himself stiffly, shook his head. "I'll see his folks, Gus."

"You get inside and stay there. That mob'll string you up."

"They won't do one thing," Slattery said calmly. The two who'd gone inside the hotel had reappeared. The others crowded in around them. "I didn't kill that kid. I'm not running from anyone." He took a step through the mud.

Loheed touched his arm. "No. You don't go, not that way." He glanced at the men, something hidden in his look. It wasn't fear, but something grudging. "You feel you have to talk to the Bromley's, you go in the back."

Slattery said hotly, "One thing about you, Sheriff. You don't push things, do you."

"Not when it won't do no good."

"Right now it would."

Gus Loheed nodded toward the restaurant alleyway as though he conveniently hadn't heard. "I'll keep them out here in the street," he said. Then,

116

without giving a chance for disagreement, he retraced his steps along the middle of the roadway.

Slattery went into the black darkness of the restaurant alleyway, watchful that someone might have come out back here to wait for him. The Ellsons, Chino and Gillman were in the gang which now moved down the street like a lynch mob to talk to Loheed. But he had no idea where MacCandles was, or where he'd spotted his man named Lewis. The storm was only a bare trace of light flashes below the southern horizon. Rain drops had changed to a fine, windy mist that plastered his clothing coldly and damply against his skin.

The hotel lobby was empty. He could hear movements in the kitchen before he reached the open doorway. Martin Bromley stood at the long iron woodstove making a pot of coffee. He looked around when Slattery entered.

"I heard about Fred, Mr. Bromley," Slattery began.

"You better leave," the hotelman told him. He spoke the words low. They seemed hollow in the emptiness of the room.

"If there's anything I can do, I'd be glad—"

The bedroom door swung open wide and Mrs. Bromley stood there. "You've done too much already," she cried. "You and your trouble! Make him leave, Martin! Make him!"

Slattery stared helplessly from the woman to her husband.

Bromley said, "Do what she wants. Don't stay

here. Please."

Slattery backed through the doorway. His father and brother, and now this boy, he thought. And Ellen Hasslett and Charlie Raine were so close to this trouble they could be next. He moved toward the registration desk, realizing exactly what he'd have to face outside, knowing from the way Loheed straddled the high fence he'd have to do it completely alone. But he never reached the porch door.

Two men waited to the left of the desk. When they appeared both held aimed carbines. Byron Foye, the huge muscled blacksmith, jerked the barrel of his Spencer rifle toward the lobby's rear door.

"Outside this way, Slattery. Quick about it."

Slattery paused, and the muzzle rose threateningly. "I'll smash you right here," Foye snarled. "Right here."

Slattery moved in front of the pair. Foye stepped close beside him, opened the door with one hand, shoved Slattery outside with the other.

The men crowded in the alley were as black as the night, only their boots and trousers visible in the shaft of lamplight thrown through the open doorway.

"You wanted trouble," a voice snarled. A hand grabbed Slattery and threw him against the wall of the building.

Matt Ellson's voice said, "Get his gun. Grab it!"

Slattery froze, feeling the bodies push in on him. He pressed the flat of his back against the solid wood, reached wildly with his right hand to grip his gun.

A man cursed and a hand slapped the reaching fingers aside. A stinging blow landed on the side of Slattery's head, straightening him where he stood. He brought up both hands to defend himself as another fist struck. Dark was all around, covered the ground, blacked the walls and roof edges, and he couldn't see who hit him. He tried to duck away to keep his balance but couldn't. An attacker had his coat open and yanked out the Colt. The throng pressed in on him, smashing, pushing, shoving at each other to get at him. A few of them yelled curses and swore in their fury.

A chopping fist pounded all feeling from Slattery's neck, another scraped skin from his cheek. Slattery lunged forward, tried to break through to the lamplight so he could see, but a vicious smash into his stomach blasted air from his lungs.

His arms reached out, attempted to catch hold of something for support. His outstretched fingers were flayed aside, and more fists joined in the pummeling. Falling, he felt his body lifted up to a standing position, heard a shrill hate-filled yell as he was punched to the muddy ground.

Hands grabbed along his entire length, arms, legs, head, body. He was pulled and held erect, then smashed back onto all fours. A warm wetness ran across his face, thick and sticky, and he gulped in the taste of his own blood. Then he was on the ground and the screaming yells seemed a long way off.

One loud, shrill somehow familiar voice wounded through the shouting. "What are you men doing? What are you doing, Ellson?"

The yelling began to break off at the rear of the mob. Slattery lay sprawled out in the darkness, but in the haze of lamplight he could see the feet of his attackers were moving back.

Matt Ellson said excitedly, "Keep out of this, Bromley."

"Get away from him," Martin Bromley ordered. A thin rumble of protest rose in the crowd. It died almost instantly.

"Hey! Hey, watch him!" a voice called. "Watch his gun!"

Then, "Get back! Back, all of you!"

Slattery pushed himself up onto one elbow. Through the tears that stung his eyes he saw Martin Bromley stood above him holding an Army Enfield rifle waist-high, aimed and ready.

"Get away from him!" Bromley was repeating. "I'll kill the first one who touches him again."

Matt Ellson called, "He killed your kid! Bromley, how can—"

"Let him stand!" the old man screamed. "You in close! Back! Back away!"

"You forgotten Freddy?" someone shouted. Another picked that up, added, "That bushwhacker grabbed Freddy and rode out with a gun on him. He had no reason to kill the kid. All he's told is rotten lies!"

A roar of agreement went up then, and the men pressed closer together, as though they intended to start on Slattery again. Slattery could only stay there, mud covered, slumped on his elbows, spitting the blood that seeped from his torn lips.

Bromley motioned the mob back with a threatening upward lift of the rifle's muzzle.

"I don't blame Slattery for any of this." Bromley spoke slowly, his voice level. "My son saw Horse Owens out back here when Bol Nye was murdered. There was another man there, too, but Freddy couldn't see him. They ran across, toward the Frontier. I—we wouldn't let him tell that in court." He breathed deeply, then added, "Now you know. You know our shame."

Silence fell, dead silence. Only the noise of feet squelching in the wet sand came from the mob. A few of those in the rear moved audibly off into the adjoining alleyways. The rest began to follow.

Bromley bent low and picked Slattery's Colt from where it had been thrown in the muck. He centered the rifle on Gillman. "Get out," he said. "Tell MacCandles we kept our boy quiet because we were afraid. There's nothing to be afraid of now. Get out!"

Without answering, Gillman backed away.

Bromley leaned close to Slattery, grasped him by the armpits to help him stand. "Careful, careful, Tom," he said. "Don't try so fast. Do it careful, Tom."

Chapter Fourteen

Ellen Hasslett hadn't gone back to her home after she'd talked to Slattery. She had stopped on the porch of the millinery shop, had watched everything that had taken place on the street. She didn't fear the dark, though it seemed she'd never been out in a night as black as this one. She could not see anyone close to her, nor could she hear any sound other than the whisper of the damp wind barely audible in the eaves of the two-story building. Now, Ellen stared at the throng of men who'd suddenly appeared from the alleyway; the Ellsons, Chino, Nate Gillman and four or five others took their time while they crossed to the Frontier Saloon. The rest hurried toward their homes. They were very silent, and she felt a sudden burning in her throat gag her. They'd done what they'd meant to do, what they'd waited for since Slattery rode in. But somehow there wasn't much satisfaction there, from the low and guarded way they talked, and from the way they split up and left each other, as if all the pride in their act was gone.

Ellen wasn't certain of exactly what she should do. If Slattery was badly hurt, he'd want to be alone. If he wasn't, MacCandles would be sure to go after him. She'd do all she could to help, but she couldn't chance getting caught in the middle of a gunfight.

"Why does he have to do everything by himself?" she muttered, letting the words sound in the darkness because she was alone. "I could've helped more. I can help now. I know I can."

She watched the two men who came along the walk toward her. One broke off at Cross Street, disappeared into the darkness there. The second, Amos Minnock who owned the harness shop, continued on in her direction.

She waited until Minnock was almost to the porch steps before she showed herself. Charlie Raine had been inside the sheriff's office. He'd looked out when the men had poured from the alleyway. Now, he left the jail with Loheed. The two crossed Center directly for the hotel.

Minnock stopped short when he caught Ellen's first step. His tall, lanky body moved to the edge of the walk. One shoe reached for the muddy street before he saw who it was.

His voice held a note of panic. "Ellen? What are you doin' out here like this?"

Ellen gave an exasperated cough, spoke softly. "What happened up there?"

"Nothing. It wasn't anythin' you'd want to see."

"You beat Slattery. The whole gang of you."

Minnock glanced around sheepishly. Charlie Raine and the sheriff had almost reached the hotel. "Better get inside," he said. "There might be trouble."

"Then Slattery isn't hurt bad." She heaved a sigh of relief. "You, they didn't hurt him."

"He's hurt. But he shouldn't've been this time. The Bromley kid held somethin' back at the trial. Maybe . . ." His stare flicked to the two men walking up the hotel stairs. "You better get inside, Ellen."

"I'll be all right."

"You better." He gazed at the lighted windows of the houses beyond them. "Anythin' comes now, you'll only be safe inside."

She gave no answer. Minnock hesitated a moment longer. Then, without another word, he stepped away and continued on to his home.

Ellen stayed where she was, watching Charlie and Loheed go past the lobby door. Jim Mac-Candles must be following their movements just as closely from the Frontier, she thought, judging by the way he had gone straight into the saloon. It was a good thing, for it promised the hidden maneuvering was ready to explode into the open. With the truth about Freddy Bromley's testimony coming out, the next few hours would have to build up to some sort of a climax. MacCandles couldn't afford to let Slattery keep moving around to ask questions.

She'd done what she should, trying to get Slattery to leave. But this way might be better. It would be decided now, once and for all. She knew how Slattery would be. Hurt or not, he'd come back fast and hard, ready to fight. She could see MacCandles, too. The party he'd used to cover himself, the people he'd had there. Mentally, she could see him, wooden-faced but seething inside. If she knew the man, he'd hide that, controlling

124

himself to the point where the tightened muscles would whiten the corners of his mouth.

She'd be needed, she knew. She'd helped this far, and she'd been needed.

Ellen moved off the porch steps and toward her house. She had held down her flushed exhilaration, forced herself to relax. She'd get out of her damp clothes and open the restaurant early. She would naturally be in a spot where she could help. Smiling in anticipation, she stepped down to the road, paying no attention to the ankle-deep mud or the filthy puddles that darkened the hem of her skirt.

Sheriff Gus Loheed looked from the closed kitchen door to Martin Bromley. "You and your wife knew this all this time," he said. "And you still let the trial go on?"

"We were thinking of the boy," Bromley answered. He shook his head at Slattery standing beside him, his coat and pants mud-soaked, boots grimy and leaving a wet puddle below his heels.

Slattery said, "Martin thinks it could have been Matt Ellson who ran into the Frontier." He brushed one hand across his right eye, swollen almost completely shut, touched the purplish-black bruise which discolored that side of his face. He drew a long breath, paying no attention to the little trickle of blood that still came from his swollen lower lip. "I'm going to find out."

"I'm not letting you stand up to that gang," Loheed said. "You won't have a chance."

"This is the first time I really have had any kind

of a chance, Sheriff."

Loheed shook his head. "You don't go out there. The minute you draw—"

"All right," Slattery said, anger riding his words. "You keep hidin' in here." He jerked the Colt from his waistband, handed it to the old cook. "You stay right here and keep hidin'." He buttoned his coat, swung around for the front door.

Charlie Raine grabbed Slattery's arm. "What in hell are you doin', Tom?"

"Stay outside the Frontier with that gun. Don't come close to me."

"No, you'll . . ." The old cook's words failed him as Slattery pulled his sleeve free and went through the doorway.

Matt Ellson was at the far end of the Frontier's bar leaning on his elbows, arms spread wide, occupying a generous expanse of the mahogany and brass. Slattery kept up a long, determined stride after he swished in the batwings. Billy Ellson, beside his brother, gave a quick, sidelong stare. Matt spoke to him, and to Chino, then casually raised a shot glass to his mouth and downed his liquor. Len McEneny had been busy washing glasses over the round wooden tub behind the counter. He stopped what he was doing, watched Slattery come up to the bar. The appearance of Sheriff Loheed behind Slattery didn't alter the bartender's fright.

Slattery felt the tense silence, saw how the eyes of the drinkers along the rails and at the tables followed him. He stopped directly opposite McEneny, leaned his long body forward on the wood.

126

He nodded to the bartender.

"Whiskey," he said. "Three fingers."

McEneny's thin lips trembled, and he seemed to shrink away from the water tub. He shook his head at Gus Loheed. "I know it's after closin' time, Sheriff. But these men come in."

"You can give me a drink," Slattery said.

The long thin face shook again. "I'm closin'. I'm sorry."

"That's all right. The law's the law." Slattery's gaze went to Matt Ellson and back to the bartender. "That night Bol Nye was killed. Horse Owens ran in here with another man right after the shooting. You remember that, Len?"

McEneny wiped a wet hand across his jaw. "I can't. No, I can't."

"You remember Horse comin' in?"

"Yeah—he come in, but I can't tell you 'bout anyone else."

Slattery nodded slightly, said in a perfectly calm voice, "Look down at Matt Ellson. I was told he was the man with Horse."

Matt Ellson muttered a Mexican obscenity. He stepped clear of the counter. Billy moved with him, staying bare inches from his brother's gunhand. Matt said, "You don't go pullin' that stuff, Slattery."

"What stuff? I just asked a question."

"You're doin' more than just askin'."

The latch of the back storeroom door snapped. When the door opened, Jim MacCandles stepped into the long saloon. Gillman and Slim Lewis, a thin, red-headed cowhand dressed in Levi's and a gray shirt, walked into position on either side of the rancher.

Slattery acted as though he hadn't noticed them. Giving another slight nod, he straightened. He touched the middle button of his coat, undid it. "You were in town that night, Matt. You'd been seen with Horse."

Matt Ellson opened his mouth to speak but Jim MacCandles answered first. "You have no right pushing my man, Slattery. Any of my men."

This was what Slattery waited for. MacCandles had come over here from the hotel, had stayed innocent and untouchable inside the storeroom while the mob had given its beating. All his cover-up was valueless now. Everyone present knew the two real enemies within the room. Slattery did not look at MacCandles, only at Matt Ellson.

"I was told it was you who ran in with Horse."

"Don't push me, Slattery." His eyes shifted to MacCandles, as if asking a question.

Slattery caught MacCandles' grimace. He said, "Go ahead, Matt, have him cover you. Bring Billy in on it too."

MacCandles said quickly, "I'm not letting you throw down on one of my men, Slattery. Sheriff, you can see what he's trying to do."

Slattery gave Loheed no time to speak. He grinned at Matt Ellson who was flushed with anger. He moved his right hand up. MacCandles sensed what was coming. He took a step closer to Matt. And in that motion, Slattery touched his coat.

Matt Ellson's gun hand streaked down and back,

whipped up with his six-gun.

"No, no, no, don't!" MacCandles yelled. One arm shot out, hit Ellson's wrist violently. The weapon, almost level, banged, spurted fire. The bullet whanged hard into the mahogany of the bar.

Ellson, knocked off balance, caught himself. "What you—"

"He isn't going to draw," MacCandles snapped. "You see that?"

Slattery stood stiff, straight, his eyes on Sheriff Gus Loheed. The relief he felt in tricking the cowhand did little to calm the shakiness in his stomach. His jaw and cheek ached, the places where he'd taken blows along his ribs and stomach and groin, all cried for rest. But he waited without moving or saying a word while the lawman drew his gun.

"I'll take that," Loheed said to Matt Ellson. The fingers of his left hand stretched for Ellson's weapon.

Ellson looked from MacCandles to Loheed. "I wasn't with Horse that night."

"You're comin' in for drawin' on an unarmed man."

Jim MacCandles' voice was hard, loud. "Loheed, you saw what Slattery pulled."

"Matt drew on Slattery," Loheed said tightly. His fingers gripped the revolver barrel, jerked it from Ellson's hand. "Right across to the jail. Now."

Still dumbfounded, Matt Ellson began to walk. Len McEneny, pasty-faced, stared bug-eyed at MacCandles. Chatter went up among the men around the tables. Billy Ellson took a hasty step after his brother and the lawman, but MacCandles reached out and stopped him.

"Mr. MacCandles," Billy began.

"Let him go," the rancher ordered. "I'll get him out."

"But Matt—"

"Shut up!" And to the rest of the cowhands, "Don't do anything. Not one thing. I'll handle this."

The rancher remained motionless, his face wooden, the corners of his mouth bitten into tight white lines, watching Slattery push past the swinging doors a step behind Loheed and Matt Ellson.

Outside Charlie Raine came close to stumbling while he hurried from where he'd watched through the window. He shoved one hand under his coat. "Here, Tom. Take your gun."

"Not now," Slattery said.

Raine's wrinkled face shot a glance over the batwings still fanning in and out. "They'll be after you, Tom. Take the gun."

"I'll take it before I get to my room," Slattery said. He didn't slow his stride, went down the porch steps and waded through the ankle-deep muck across toward the restaurant.

Chapter Fifteen

Slattery paused at the mouth of the restaurant alleyway. He surveyed the length of the street in the few seconds it took Charlie Raine to step in next to him. One man, Chino, had come onto the Frontier porch. He'd stopped at the top of the steps, his head bent as he cupped his hands while he struck a match to a cigarette. Most of the lights which had been on in the west end houses had gone off; their windows, porches and doors were black and still. The sky was not as dark as it had been. The clouds had started to break away, and toward the north stars glittered here and there with cold, distant brilliance.

"I'll take the Colt, Charlie," said Slattery. "You go ahead back to your place."

Raine's thin lined face moved back and forth. "I c'n stay out in the barn and watch. I c'n get a rifle."

"No, Charlie. I've got to do this alone."

"They'll be after you, the whole gang of them," the old cook said, his voice rising. "All I'll do is watch. I c'n warn you when anyone shows."

Slattery gripped the Colt's butt, said easily, "If you were out back I'd have to watch out for you. When they come, I want to be sure I'm shooting at the right people. Go ahead, Charlie, right out here, so they'll know you're not in on this."

Slattery hesitated only a minute longer until the old man moved off, limping slowly along the walk. Then he slipped into the thick blackness of the alleyway. MacCandles would come after him; he had to now that one of his men was locked up. There hadn't been time for him or his gunhands to get around behind the restaurant, nor did Slattery think the rancher would try so soon. He'd wait, pick his time. But, because he couldn't be absolutely sure, Slattery walked slowly once he was close to the alley's foot. He could hear no sound except the cold dampness of the river wind breathing past the corners of the buildings.

The key was in the sand at the side of the steps, and inside, the kitchen lamp was on the table where he'd left it. Slattery didn't light a match until he was at the stairway. He went up to the second floor cautiously. The men who'd stand with MacCandles in the open were outside, but he had no way of knowing exactly who else was close enough to the rancher to go after him in here.

Slattery set the lamp on the dresser top. He laid his blanket roll on the bed and opened it. He had a change of a shirt and underclothes, but he'd have to clean the mud off his coat and pants and boots before he lay down.

He took off his coat, stepped to the window while he unbuttoned his shirt. North, the sky was clearing fast, and the stars gave enough illumination to define the line of vast stretch of prairie where it met the horizon. It lay like a silent, black, still sea, cut by the thin track of the railroad where

132

it stretched out endlessly from beyond the height of the redwood water tank and the roundhouse.

Chino was gone from the Frontier porch. Center was empty. After watching two minutes, Slattery saw a flipped cigarette trace a tiny rocket path in the saloon alleyway. He edged away from the curtain, touched the tender bruised skin of his mouth. He'd wash and catch some sleep while he waited. They'd be after him, and there would be four or five at least when they came. He hoped it would be before daybreak, for he didn't want either of the only two people who'd helped him, mixed into a gunfight. He'd leave here and get his horse and draw MacCandles out onto the flat before he'd chance letting either Charlie Raine or Ellen Hasslett get caught in the middle.

Nate Gillman, leaning with his left shoulder pressed against the Frontier clapboards, had watched Slattery's shadow pull back from the window. Nate didn't know whether or not Slattery had seen his cigarette. He didn't care. This whole damn trouble was coming to a showdown, and now that Matt Ellson was locked up, Nate was the fastest gun MacCandles had. Anxious and restless, he didn't care if Slattery noticed him. He was out here to watch and see Slattery did nothing Jim MacCandles didn't know about, just like Chino waited behind the restaurant barn. If Slattery came out this way, Nate would welcome the fight.

Up in the center room above the restaurant porch, the lamplight dimmed and then flickered out. Gillman grinned. He'd be damned if Mac-

Candles hadn't been right after all. He'd figured Slattery would use some time to rest. That MacCandles! In the two years he'd worked for Circle M, Gillman couldn't remember once Mac-Candles hadn't out-guessed his opposition. The talk he'd spread had kept the town so on edge the people were ready to lynch Slattery the minute he rode in. Even the way he'd stayed inside the Frontier an hour ago had kept his name clear of the beating. And that beating would slow Slattery down, no matter how he tried to rest.

Gillman fingered his shirt pocket for makings but then he dropped his hand. Somewhere to his left, he thought he'd heard a sound. He listened—nothing. Gillman did not reach for his tobacco and paper. Once Slattery showed, he'd act fast. Not being quick enough had been Horse Owens' mistake. And Matt Ellson had let Slattery fool him. Gillman didn't fear Slattery, yet he wasn't going to underestimate him either.

The noise was there on his left again. Nate Gillman turned his head, listened. When he saw the figure coming across the dark saloon porch, he edged deeper into the blackness of the alleyway.

It was Charlie Raine. He could tell by the limp. Crouched down low, the old fool headed for the spot where Gillman had just been standing.

Shoes splashed mud and Raine stepped into the darkness. The glare of the close street lamp reflected on something in his hand.

Gillman took one long step, gripped the old man's arm. Raine whirled, a sudden terrified gasp deep in his throat. Completely shocked, he gave no fight when Gillman's free hand reached down and grabbed the revolver from his fingers.

"Get back there," Gillman snarled. He shoved hard, hurled Raine against the wall. Off balance, Raine's bad leg slid on the slippery earth and he crashed to the ground.

"Stay there," Gillman ordered. He leaned with the flat of his back flush to the building, studied the middle window across the street.

"What're you goin' to do?" Raine asked.

"Shut up! Just shut up and stay there."

Raine sloshed in the mud while he pushed himself up. With little feeling in the game leg he almost stumbled again as he stood.

Gillman watched in silence, doubtful about how to handle the old man. It was around three, and he'd have to hold him here too long. He heard Raine's movements, low and slow, and the problem solved itself. The old fool was trying to get away through the back, inching deeper and deeper into the alley.

Gillman let Raine get halfway to the end before he acted. Bending low, he ran back. He seized both bony shoulders and flung him onto the ground. Holding the barrel of the gun he'd taken, he struck with the butt once, twice, and again. Raine was limp and unconscious when the gunman straightened.

For a full minute Gillman waited, his body absolutely still, listening for anyone who might have heard. After he was positive, he broke the revolver and shook the bullets into the mud. Then he walked back to the alley's mouth and watched and waited.

The living room of Ellen Hasslett's home was high-ceilinged and long, with thick flowered drapes across the wide double windows. Living alone as she did, she'd wanted the best, and she'd spent lavishly on her New England-made Colonial furniture and sofa and chairs. Her greatest pride was her bedroom upstairs, but tonight she hadn't even changed into her night clothes.

She'd waited here at the window, the drape pulled aside, watching the business district. She couldn't see the porch of the Frontier Saloon, yet she knew exactly what had gone on inside. She'd stepped onto her front walk and had stopped Len McEneny when he came hurrying past to his home. The fact that Slattery was up in the room above the restaurant meant she'd have a part in what would happen. She gloated over that, depended on it.

The hall grandfather clock chimed the hour. Ellen listened, counted.

"Three," she said aloud. "He should be here. He'll come. He has to come."

She waited exactly nine more minutes before the familiar click of a key in the kitchen door broke the silence of the house.

She turned toward the doorway, heard the solid, sure footsteps. Jim MacCandles came into the room.

He was smiling, but his handsome face was dead serious. "I knew you'd be up," he said.

"You did?" She kept her manner cool, letting

him know he wasn't going to smooth over everything with just words.

His smile softened. He stopped inches from her, his gaze tentative on the firm swell of her dress where her bosom rose and fell with her breathing. "You knew I hadn't planned to come in until Slattery left."

"I didn't know about the party you were having at your house."

He stared at her, then broke into a quiet laugh. "That? That's why you're like this. It was the best way I knew of to have witnesses." One hand rose to stroke her arm.

"Barbara Forsythe was there, Jim. I know she was there."

"Of course she was there." His fingers felt her whole body stiffen. He didn't let go, simply held on lightly. "Her father is the biggest rancher on the south bank. I do business with him. I've told you there's nothing more to it than that."

"You were out there last Saturday. You were!"

"And I told you Sunday night when I came. She means nothing, Ellie. You're the only one." He drew her closer, kissed the top of her head, then ran his lips along the nape of her neck. "She isn't one-tenth the woman you are."

His arms tightened, hands gripping her supple back. Her head raised and she came up to him, her lips ready, willing under his. She linked her fingers behind his neck, pressed the entire length of her body against him.

MacCandles' hands loosened slightly and he kissed her cheeks, her neck. "Ellie," he murmured.

"It'll be over soon. This morning."

"I just wasn't sure, Jim. I'd done everything you wanted. The people hate me for taking Slattery in, but I did, so I could watch him the way you wanted. I told Gillman Slattery was going out to your ranch. Then, I heard Barbara was out there."

"You know why. There's no worry there."

"But I can't help it. I—I was willing to do anything to help, Jim. Anything."

"I know," he said. He lifted her chin with his hand, stared down into her face. "He's up in your room now. I've got to get him before he gets Matt Ellson into court. He trusts you. You can get him where I want him."

She studied MacCandles evenly. "Not for a killing, Jim. I went along with everything in my restaurant, but you know how I feel about the rest."

"Ellen, I've got to settle this once and for all."

"But not by killing. Not if I'm going to have anything to do with it."

"Ellen."

She drew back from his embrace. "I told you, Jim. There must be some other way." Her voice softened, "He isn't a bad man. Whatever he's done he's been forced—"

"Okay. Okay," MacCandles said, cutting across her words impatiently. "We can do it without shooting. If you'll help."

"You promise, Jim?"

MacCandles looked at her in silence, trying to keep a check on his temper. He needed her and couldn't chance a break with her, not right now.

138

She'd been in on too much tonight, had been too close to him too many nights for the past three years. "I'll be satisfied to get him clear of town until Matt's let out. I'll talk to the judge in the morning. But I've got to have Slattery before then."

He turned to face the kitchen at the loud knocking on the door. He stepped away from her, walked through to the back entrance.

Billy Ellson waited on the stoop. "It's almost three-thirty, Mr. MacCandles," he began. "If we're gonna help Matt, we better move."

"That's all you wanted me for?" MacCandles said coldly.

"Mr. MacCandles, my brother's locked up. Slattery could figure some way to keep him in there. I don't think—"

"You're damned right you don't think," MacCandles snapped. "You get out with the rest. I'll be out and tell you what to do."

Billy Ellson pulled away from the closing door. MacCandles swore softly to himself, thinking of the boy barging in on him like that. Then the rancher calmed. What the kid felt was natural. Gillman, Chino and Lewis were just as much on edge, keyed up and ready to explode. The waiting had built up a drive for a fight that wouldn't hurt their coordination, so in a way, it was a good thing. All he had to do was get Slattery in a position for them to hit. It didn't matter how he did it, what he had to do or say to Ellen.

MacCandles walked back into the long room. "All right," he said to Ellen. "We'll do this your way." He circled one long arm around her shoulders, stared her toward the hall stairway.

"Not now," she said, slowing. "This isn't right, now."

MacCandles laughed, tightened his arm. "It's right, Ellie," he said. "You don't usually open up 'till a half hour before daybreak. We've got time, plenty of time to talk this whole thing out."

Chapter Sixteen

Sheriff Gus Loheed had waited between the open doorway and the window of his office for the last three hours. Matt Ellson had fallen asleep around four, but there was no sleep for the lawman. Instead, he paced the small square room, constantly aware of the weight of the holstered six-gun around his hips. He'd put out the overhead coal oil lamp, knowing he'd see better in the dark and that he'd make less of a target in here if MacCandles meant to stop him from interfering with his plans for Slattery. Loheed was bone tired. His back and legs ached from being on his feet so long. His stomach growled from lack of food. He watched the windows above the restaurant porch, wondered what Slattery was thinking. A law officer who straddled the road and thought only of himself deserved nothing but hate and contempt, but Tom had really shown neither so far.

Sure, Loheed thought, he'd kept Center from being turned into a battlefield. But now, with Freddy Bromley lying in the undertaker's, it didn't seem like much of an accomplishment. He stood looking toward the sky, almost clear of clouds in this last hour before sunrise. The countless dots of stars twinkled like icy flakes of light against the blackness. The river breeze had a good smell, cool in the freshness of the night air.

The muscles in Loheed's legs became strained from the way he stood, and he shifted his stance. He rubbed the palm of his hands down along the legs of his trousers, wiped off the clammy sweat. He glanced west and east along the street, then up at the window. When he'd taken Matt Ellson in, he'd been positive MacCandles would act. He was still sure, but not certain exactly when. He'd been up twenty-four hours, or near to it. He remembered seeing Ellie Hasslett turning the lights on inside her place when he'd come from his own house yesterday.

He wondered about Katie and the kids. He'd given strict orders concerning what they were to do once Slattery rode in. He should've sent word to Katie. She'd be in a terrible state once more gunfire started. But she'd keep the kids inside. He didn't have a worry there; his worry was out in front here, more in what he could not see.

A sound creaked somewhere beyond the back door. Loheed turned with quick silence. His hand fell to the butt of his six-gun, slid the weapon free of its holster. His readiness, the sudden encouragement of the hardwood grip under his palm, surprised him slightly. He moved to one side, stepped fast toward the door.

"Gus." The word penetrated the wood, low and weak, but he knew the voice.

"What is it, Charlie?"

"Let me in. In, Gus."

Loheed snapped the key in the lock. He jerked the door open. The six-gun in his hand was held level, cocked for anyone who might try to get in by using Charlie Raine as a shield.

The elderly cook pushed the door shut behind him. In the thick blackness Loheed couldn't see him, but he could smell mud, could hear Raine's clothing and shoes drip water as he moved.

"What's the matter, Charlie?"

Raine leaned against the door. His heavy breathing stirred the darkness while he told about Nate Gillman, ending with, "I just come 'round now. He wasn't there any more. He must've took the gun when he went."

Loheed picked a sulphur match from his pocket, flicked it into flame with his fingernail. Raine said quickly, "No, no, Gus. Keep it out in case they're watching."

Loheed blew against the flame, seeing in its moment of brightness the swelling on the left side of Raine's head, and his muddy clothes. "You two were alone," he said. "You wouldn't have a witness?"

"If I had one, what good would it do?" Raine made the statement wearily. "You pick up Nate, MacCandles'll have him out as soon as he pays Matt Ellson's fine."

"You could make charges. I'll pick him up."

"You go after any one of MacCandles' men now, Gus, they'll make damn short work of gettin' you out of the way. They'd have a turkey shoot with Tom Slattery."

For a long minute Loheed didn't speak. He stared at Raine's form, a hazy silhouette blocking the panes of the street window. The lawman had

143

words phrased in his mind but he forgot them when he saw someone walking past the lamp in front of the barber shop. He moved quickly to the window.

Daybreak was coming slowly. With its first sign, the blurred squares of false fronts had become individual shapes against the brightening sky. Alleyways seemed darker, blacker, and doorways seemed deep enough to hide a man. The figure was in plain sight, unmistakable in its coat and shawl. Neither man spoke a word as they watched Ellen Hasslett start onto the restaurant steps.

Raine watched Ellen insert her key in the lock. "She'll get caught in it, Gus," he said. "I better go across."

"No, hold it," Gus Loheed told him. The lawman swung around and walked to the gunrack. He picked two long-barrelled Winchester 73 carbines from their places and handed one to Raine. Then he moved to the rolltop desk.

He opened the middle drawer and brought out a box of .44 shells. He passed a handful to the old cook, then stepped into the doorway. Once he was in plain view of anyone who could be watching from the street, he loaded the weapon, snapped it shut.

His eyes were on Ellen Hasslett opening the door. Loheed said across his shoulder, "Lock up behind me soon as I go."

"Look, Gus. I better go too."

"Stay right here," Loheed said, his voice tight showing the strain now. "No matter what happens, I'm not losing my prisoner."

He stepped onto the walk, started across Center. Above him, in the thick shadows of the hotel porch, Ellen Hasslett was out of sight inside and the door shut behind her.

Tom Slattery was awakened by the sound of footsteps which seemed to be approaching his room. Instantly his hand reached under his pillow and came out with the Colt revolver. The room was in darkness. Pushing himself up onto one elbow, he stared straight at the door, listened, then sat up on the edge of the bed. His head and jaw and stomach were stiff, ached while he moved, but he gave that no attention. The noises were low, as though whoever worked about downstairs was trying to mask what he was doing.

Slattery opened the bedroom door slowly, quietly, his body held to the side in case shooting broke out.

A shadow moved about in the lighted kitchen. Slattery's finger tightened on the trigger. Then Ellen Hasslett, busy tying a bow in her apron, appeared at the bottom of the staircase.

Her pretty face was troubled, concerned for him. "I didn't wake you, did I?" she said.

Slattery grinned and started to walk down. "I slept longer than I figured I would," he said. He halted beside her, nodded toward the window. Light was beginning to filter down into the yard, giving the barn and trees hazy shapes, as yet gray and colorless, but even as he looked the barn roof seemed to become clearer. "You believe in getting in here early."

Ellen's stare had been on the window, still pensive and worried. Now, she watched him. "I'm here at this time every morning. I have to do my baking before the railroad crews stop off for breakfast." Her stare switched with the final word, became glued to the dining room doors.

Slattery was already in motion. He'd caught the knocking in there. His left hand waved her back from the doorway. "Over behind the stove," he said. "Stay right there."

He edged one door open, saw the shadow of a man standing outside. The knocks came again, shook the glass.

"Loheed," Slattery said. "I'll let him in."

Ellen gave a quick glance, a flick of her head toward the window. As quickly, her eyes returned to him. "I'll go in with you." She took a key from her apron pocket, walked past the double doors into the large room.

Gus Loheed held the Winchester carbine in both hands, businesslike, and his mustached face was deadly serious. He was aware of the Colt revolver that jutted from Slattery's waistband but made no mention of it.

"You goin' to stay here, Tom?" he asked.

"I have to appear in court against Matt Ellson."

"I mean in here." He turned to Ellen. "You're goin' to let him stay."

"Yes. He hasn't done anything wrong, Sheriff."

A slight raising of Loheed's square jaw brought silence. "Then you should get back to your house 'til this is over. Here, I'll walk out with you, and Charlie Raine can take you home."

146

Ellen, frowning, looked grim. "Does there have to be a fight, Sheriff? Can't this be settled another way?"

Loheed shook his head. "Not unless Tom decides to leave. I can't make him, seein' as he hasn't started any trouble on his own. I don't know now as I want to stop him. You come with me, so you'll be good and safe when he goes out."

Ellen's stare went from the lawman to Slattery. "I won't stay," she said through tight lips. "But I want to talk to Tom first."

Loheed studied the man and woman for a few moments. Then, slowly, his head moved up and down, his eyes on Slattery. "Do it fast," he said. "It'll be light enough in five, ten minutes. You know what that'll mean."

Nodding, Slattery followed the lawman to the door. He locked it, tested it before he pulled out the key and handed it to Ellen. "I'll get your coat," he told her. "You'd better go with him before it gets too light."

Ellen followed him into the kitchen. "This trouble doesn't have to end in a gunfight. There must be another way."

"There isn't," Slattery said. He took her blue coat from the hook, held it so she could slip her arms into the sleeves. He could see how she stood, her body tense, her whole concentration on the yard. The eastern horizon showed a band of whiteness, and the slanted roof of the barn was lighter than on the dark western side. "MacCandles can't afford to let Ellson go before a judge, not with the questions I'll be asking."

147

"But there must be another way." There was still a tone of hope in her words. "Without you or anyone else getting killed."

"No, MacCandles can't chance anything in this. He knows that. And that he has to act."

"MacCandles," Ellen said. "I've never seen that Jim MacCandles has to do anything if he doesn't really want to!"

"He does this time," Slattery said. "There was another man with Horse Owens the night Nye was murdered. They had to run across Center to get to the Frontier. If Ellson is on that stand long enough, someone will remember seeing him. Mac-Candles can't chance that."

"You hate him, don't you?" Ellen asked.

Slattery wondered at the irrelevent question. In the quiet he saw how she unconsciously kept her ear to the window and the yard. "No, not that kind of hate," he said. "But I hate what he stands for. I hate what he's done to the people here. They were in a state of mind where they'd accept a murder, Freddy Bromley's murder, and not feel they were part of it." He took a step toward the dining room. "They know MacCandles is coming after me. You've seen how they accept that."

Ellen didn't move. Her troubled expression was unchanged. "I don't know about the street, Tom. If MacCandles comes . . ." Her eyes went to the yard. "I could go out the back. Once I get away from the yard, I'll be safer behind the buildings."

Slattery nodded. "I'll go a way with you. Walk just as fast as you can outside."

She waited beside him while he turned the key. When she went to go ahead of him, Slattery

148

warned, "Wait." He stepped onto the stoop in front of her, surveyed the silent gray-darkness of the sandy yard, the closed door of the outhouse and the barn. No sound or movement there, or in either of the adjoining yards.

Once his boot touched the ground, Slattery paused to let Ellen step in beside him. "Stay next to the building," he said quietly. "Stop at the alley."

"No, Tom. I'll be safer if we go past the barn," Ellen said. She hung back, pulled him away from the wall. "Please. I'll feel safer, Tom."

At that instant both high doors of the barn swung out wide, wood creaking loudly, rust from the hinges tearing the silence like a wild screech. Two dark figures stood there, arms raised, rifles aimed. Another appeared to the left of the barn, a fourth from behind the outhouse.

"Down," Slattery whispered drawing his Colt. "Stay here. I'll lead them off."

"They won't shoot, Tom," Ellen said. "Just go with them and they won't shoot. They only want to hold you until Matt's let out."

Jim MacCandles' voice spoke from the barn doorway. It was calm and hard, loud enough to be heard in the yard but not to carry out into Center.

"Step away from him, Ellie. Slow now." And to the others, a little louder, tighter, "Soon as she's clear, open up. Cut him down right where he is."

Chapter Seventeen

Ellen Hasslett was stunned, frozen where she stood. "Jim, no! Not this!" She backed toward Slattery, her voice suddenly dry, shaken with disbelief. "No, Jim! No!"

MacCandles edged to the right, closed in with the others. The sun was coming up, clean and white behind the four, making their faces clear to Slattery. MacCandles' voice filled the silence, sounded assured, casual, almost affectionate.

"Come on, Ellie. Quick. This way."

"No! No! He isn't bad." Twisting around, her long dress making an audible whish as it slapped the ground, she gestured wildly at Slattery. "Run! Get out! Get awa . . ."

The sentence never finished. The weapon in MacCandles' hands cut her off in the middle of the word, two quick shots triggered together. Ellen's surprised, pain-filled scream was loud and shrill, but it ceased instantly as she began to drop headlong to the ground.

Crouching, bent forward, Slattery reached out his left hand to catch her, but she fell away from him. He heard the high whine of a passing bullet, the loud, snapping whip-like crack of the steel slug smashing, penetrating the clapboards. Gillman, Chino, and Billy Ellson, momentarily shocked at the shooting of the woman, hadn't fired. It was only a fraction of a second, the time of a heartbeat, but the hesitation gave Slattery a chance for life. He threw himself to the right, got off a shot at Gillman's squat, heavy-built figure while he took the first stride.

Gillman gave out a high cry of pain. MacCandles yelled, "Get him. What are you waiting for?" He fired a third and fourth time at Slattery, bent low, charging for the entrance of the alleyway.

Slattery heard the whine of the bullets, felt one pull at his coattail while it tore through. The three other guns pounded as he made a long dive for the restaurant corner. Steel-jacketed slugs whapped into the mud around him, ahead of him. He struck a puddle with a loud splash, held the Colt clear so it wouldn't get clogged and jam. Rolling fast, sliding his body wildly, he was almost to the sharp jutting corner.

The bullet struck his left shoulder, gave more momentum to his roll while it bore in and ripped out along the bone.

There was no pain at first. All feeling was gone. His mind was working furiously, hearing the yells that came from MacCandles, the shots, the thumping pound of boots closing in. A slug smashed the wood inches above his head, reverberated in the clapboard but didn't penetrate the thick skeletal timber. MacCandles' tall figure was coming around wide from the barn for a clear shot. Slattery lay on his right side, raised the Colt, fired.

MacCandles stopped in mid-stride, an incredulous hateful look spreading across his face. He set both feet down flat, leveled the carbine's muzzle lower at Slattery.

Slattery heard the scramble of running footsteps behind him in the alleyway, and the loud crack of a rifle somewhere on Center. He twisted his body to the left, rolled in that direction. MacCandles' weapon flashed and the bullet missed, bare inches from Slattery's head.

Slattery pushed onto his left side, fought to regain balance to raise his gun for a shot. The white-hot pain hit him then, driving like a pulse beat throughout his entire body, squeezing the breath from him. His fingers lost all their strength. The Colt slipped from his grip.

He stiffened, leaned onto his right elbow to keep from falling flat on his face, hearing the thump of Billy Ellson's and Chino's boots coming in behind MacCandles, the kicking splash of someone running behind him up the alleyway.

MacCandles was yards away, wounded but still straight, his tall body blotting out the sunlight and the height of the barn behind him. He was cursing, slowly and distinctly. "You lost, Slattery. They can't do . . ."

MacCandles never heard the shot that sent a bullet ripping into his heart. He died instantly.

The blast of the gun exploding so close behind him pounded in Slattery's eardrums. Gus Loheed splashed mud onto his hands as he ran past. Chino, coming into view, fired his Winchester low. Dirty water erupted at Loheed's boots. The lawman didn't shoot. He centered his weapon on Chino's head.

"Hold it! Right there, Chino!"

Chino dropped the Winchester down in front of him, threw both hands above his head. Billy Ellson, close behind him, stopped, then started to run again, going away this time.

Slattery was up on one knee, controlling the intense pain and nausea his movements had brought on. From the distance came the faint confusion of excited shouting.

"Billy. Stop, Billy!" Loheed was yelling. He had his carbine pressed to his shoulder. Yet, he didn't shoot. "Stop, Billy!"

Slattery had his Colt in hand now. He felt stronger while he stood. He gripped his shoulder with his left hand. Loheed back-stepped toward him.

"Billy's headin' for the street," the lawman said. "I'll get him."

"I'll head him off, Gus. You take care of Chino and the rest."

Slattery began to run down the alleyway, then had to slow to a walk when pain grew in his shoulder and slashed along his side. Loud talk filled Center. A town man had appeared at the alley mouth, then another.

Both men drew back when Slattery reached them. Slattery stepped across the walk to go into the street, almost daylight bright. The majority of the storekeepers and their wives were out, and the railroad crew who'd run up from the roundhouse. A few stepped forward, rifles and hand guns in plain view, but they halted when they saw how Slattery pointed his Colt their way. Slattery moved

153

past them into the middle of the road where most of the crowd had bulged out from the restaurant porch to make a wide semicircle around the body of Slim Lewis. Charlie Raine stood beside the dead man.

"MacCandles had him spotted here to cut Gus down," the old cook said when Slattery reached him. Raine shook the carbine he held. "He didn't see me in the jail."

"You see Billy Ellson out here?" Slattery asked.

Raine shook his head. A woman in the rear of the gathering called, "Billy crossed near the jeweler's. He ran around behind on that side."

Slattery broke into a run then, toward the jail. He'd taken two strides through the parting crowd when the single shot came, loud in its nearness, blasting inside the sheriff's office.

Billy Ellson's bullet had shattered the rear lock of the sheriff's office, and now he threw open the door. He ran in, moving with jerky strides, his eyes on the iron-barred entrance to the cell block. In the closest cubicle, his brother Matt, a shocked expression on his face, pressed himself against the vertical bars. "What in hell you doin', kid? Get out of here."

"Don't worry," Billy answered. He'd reached the barred door, gripped it and pulled. It was locked. He stared at his older brother. "Don't worry, Matt, I'll have you out of here." He yanked again, a bit nervous this time. The door didn't budge.

Billy whirled on his bootheels to the key rack.

154

Every hook on the pine board was empty.

Matt said, "Get out, kid. They'll come in. Don't wait! Just get out!"

Billy didn't seem to hear. Nervously, fearfully, he stepped to the desk and jerked out the middle drawer. No keys there! The shouting in the street was loud in the room, but he paid no attention. He'd come in to free his brother. That was his only plan. He had no other plan except to unlock the cell and let Matt out. Matt, who'd taken care of him all his life, who'd been mother and father to him. MacCandles was dead, but they could get away, him and Matt. The second drawer held no keys, nor did the third. Using one hand was too slow. Billy laid his six-gun on the desk top, then pulled at the remaining two drawers together.

"Go ahead! Get out!" Matt screamed. His face was swollen red where he crushed himself against the iron bars. "They're comin'! Get out!"

"No! MacCandles is dead! We've got to . . ."

Slattery was in the doorway, his big shoulders bent, one hand covered with blood where he gripped his collar bone, the Colt in his hand centered on Billy's chest. "Bring your hands up," he ordered. "Slow now."

Billy straightened, the wild, fear-filled expression dug into the lines of his face. He hesitated looking down at the six-gun on the desktop.

"No, Billy! No!" Matt screamed. "Don't try it!"

Billy shook his head quickly. "They'll hang you, Matt." He could see others crowding toward the walk. Sheriff Loheed was there, bringing Chino in. And Charlie Raine with a carbine. Billy's right hand began to rise. "They'll hang you, Matt!"

"No! Please, no, Billy!" Matt watched Slattery. "Don't shoot him, Slattery! He's only a kid! He didn't have nothin' to do with Nye's killin'."

Slattery took a single step forward, the Colt just eight feet from Billy Ellson's chest. "You were there, Matt?" he said. "You and Horse?"

"Yes. Yes. But Horse shot him. I'll tell that in court. Don't kill the kid. Please!"

Slattery still kept moving, was almost to the desk. "Step back, Bill. You can get out of this easier than the rest. Don't try. Matt, you'll admit you set up my father and Joe."

"I'll tell the whole thing." He spoke loud enough for Loheed and the men who crowded the doorway to hear. "MacCandles had it set up. He sent his two gunhands to get you. Billy, don't. You had nothing to do with that. Don't!"

Billy's fingers were inches from the six-gun. Slattery reached the desk, dropped his bloody left hand and swept the weapon to the floor.

"That's it, Bill," he said quietly. "Just move back. Easy now."

Behind Slattery, Gus Loheed drew the cell keys from his pocket. He kept his carbine on Chino, said to Charlie Raine, "Lock them up. Put Billy in with Matt."

Raine accepted the keys, motioned the prisoners to the door.

Slattery looked past the sheriff. The men in the doorway had turned around and talked among themselves. Their faces were no longer hostile.

They were stunned by what they'd heard, realizing their own guilt in the beatings they'd given him. The way they'd been used by MacCandles was a blow. It was taking time for them to absorb the shock.

Loheed said, "Ellie Hasslett's dead, Matt. Chino says she was helpin' MacCandles."

"Not all the way. Not at the very end." He exhaled deeply, laid the Colt on the desk. "Thanks for that out there, Gus. I'll be back and give you the whole story."

Slattery walked to the doorway. In the east the sun was a huge reddish-orange disk above the rim of the horizon. The sky was bright blue, and the broad length of flat was filled with liquid shining light. The town men, not speaking now, watched Slattery. He said nothing to them while he surveyed the length of Center. One by one, and in twos and threes, they turned away on the walks and headed off in all directions.

Slattery stepped down into the street. His legs dragged, and there was a steady slow throbbing along his shoulder and arm. He felt very tired. Gus Loheed called his name from the jail doorway, but Slattery neither glanced around nor stopped. The sheriff walked quickly to catch up. His unshaven mustached face looked darker, harder in the bright sunlight.

"You better have your own guns, Tom," he said. "I'll bring them up to your room."

Slattery gazed toward the townspeople who still lined the opposite walk watching something that went on in the hotel alleyway. The few men who

157

held weapons paid no attention to him.

"No. I'll get them when I come over to the jail."

The onlookers had made an opening at the alleyway mouth. Four men came out carrying Jim MacCandles' spread-eagled body. Two more appeared directly behind them at the head of a stretcher. Ellen Hasslett lay with her hands folded across her chest. The bullet had killed her instantly, Slattery knew, so she hadn't suffered. He was glad of this, but felt nothing else for her.

Any feeling he'd had for Ellen had been blown apart the moment he'd realized she'd led him outside to MacCandles. Slattery's fingers gripped his wounded shoulder tighter, and blood seeped along the knuckles.

"I'll be over," he said quietly. "I'll be ridin' out soon as Doc fixes me up."

"There'll be someone lookin' into the way MacCandles got his land, Tom. Some money'll be comin' back."

Slattery nodded. "I'll use some to have Pa and Joe moved, and for a stone. Charlie Raine can have the rest," he said. "The restaurant should be his."

Nodding, the lawman was silent while Slattery continued on along the roadway.

Gus Loheed didn't move until Slattery was out of the business district and almost to Doctor Gingras' house. A few of those who were still outside had their guns with them. Loheed's eyes rested on them for a second, then he went onto the walk and called through the doorway to the cell block.

"Charlie, will you stay 'till I get back?"

"Yuh, Gus." Raine came into the office.

The old cook stopped in the doorway, watched the sheriff walk directly across Center to the men near the restaurant alley. Loheed spoke to them, and the ones who carried guns held them out to him. Loheed took the weapons, tucked the long-barreled rifle under his arm and jammed two hand guns into his waistband. The Gunnison sheriff said a last few brisk words to the men. They nodded their heads, then walked away together, quiet and serious, toward their homes.

Steven C. Lawrence was born Lawrence Murphy in Brockton, Massachusetts. He was educated at Massachusetts Maritime Academy and earned a Bachelor's degree and Master's degree in journalism at Boston University. For thirty years he taught English in Brockton. He began his career as an author of Western fiction with *The Naked Range*, published in 1956 by Ace Books, followed by two of his most notable novels, *Saddle Justice* (Fawcett, 1957) and *Brand Of A Texan* (Fawcett, 1958). He is perhaps best known for his Tom Slattery series, beginning with *Slattery* (Ace, 1961). In this first book, Slattery returns from five years in a federal prison after being framed for a crime he didn't commit. After avenging himself, Slattery went on to a new adventure in *Bullet Welcome For Slattery* (Ace, 1961) in which he gets involved with smuggling over the border between Texas and Mexico. Some of the best entries in this series are *North To Montana* (Nordon, 1975) where Slattery faces treachery in Calligan Valley at the end of a long cattle drive and *Day Of The Comancheros* (Nordon, 1977) where Slattery finds a woman raped, beaten, and left to die in the desert. Generally, the Steven C. Lawrence Western novels, as George Kelley noted in *Twentieth Century Western Writers* (St. James Press, 1991), are "filled with thrilling adventures based on historical fact and solid plotting.".